D1558835

Mom, Pop, and Shawn, you continue to remind me of all the things in life that are most important, especially during the toughest times. Kathleen Pernick, Leah Spanopoulos, Glen Shilling, and Cathy Rozenberg, without knowing that my children were in your embrace, this endeavor would never have made it past the first page. Shirley Dobie and Janna Colaco, you watered a seed that I had long forgotten I'd ever planted. Una Jackman, your confidence in me, as an author, has changed the way I see myself. Jay Alix, without your careful protection and your generous spirit, I have no idea where I would be today.

Spenny, Remy, Daphne, and Michael, you make my dreams come true, including this one. Your patience and love mean more to me than you will ever know.

Love you all,
Denelle

Prologue

Quietly and calmly, she let her clothes slip to the floor. As water rushed into the bathtub, she picked up her clothing and folded it neatly, laying it gently on the tiled countertop next to the tub. She observed her naked body in the mirror and tried not to think about his lie. In sixteen years, he had never lied. Maybe she read too much into it. Maybe she shouldn't take it personally. He was, after all, allowed to spend time alone.

She opened the medicine cabinet behind the mirror and pushed a few things around until she found what she needed. As she slipped one foot into the hot water and then the other, she dipped her slender body into the water, letting the heat embrace her skin. She rested her head against the wall behind her and closed her eyes, inhaling the relaxing smell of the lavender bath salts.

She smiled faintly as she lifted the razor and rested it against her wrist. She was just so tired. The combat of her existence never seemed to relent and there was no longer any fight left in her. She saw him as her last hope, and it seemed that now she was even losing him. She pushed the blade into her arm and squeezed her eyes closed as she felt the burn as it sliced through her. She clenched her jaw as she felt the razor part her flesh. She burdened everyone, including him, it seemed. This was the right thing. It helped everyone. It was better this way. The burn of salt water entering the gaping wound took her breath away. It still didn't distract her from the memory of today.

When she'd asked him to go to the bridge with her to swim in the creek, just like they had every day since the weather had finally warmed up, he'd told her he wasn't in the mood. About an hour later she'd decided to go anyway, by herself. As she walked, she'd wondered why he didn't want to go, but brushed it aside. As the bridge came into view, she'd noticed someone sitting there. That was unusual; the bridge was off the beaten path and somewhat abandoned even. Within a few more steps, she'd realized that he was there. He had decided to go anyway, just not with her.

She closed her eyes as she realized this is what he wanted, and drifted into unconsciousness.

Chapter 1

Brianna pulled her polyester shorts over her thin hips and noticed her hands shook a bit as she reached up to smooth her hair into a ponytail. Even gossiping with her friends wasn't as fun as it usually was. Not that she ever looked forward to phys. ed., but today dread pooled in her stomach. Her best friend Julia's voice carried across the locker room as she gave her rundown of who was going with whom to the dance on Friday. Julia prided herself on being the highest authority of the juiciest gossip in school. Brianna just couldn't muster up enough enthusiasm to care about Julia's report today.

She'd never been a particularly athletic child, making gym class her least favorite anyway. She expected to do a lot of running for the planned basketball drills, but running had been miserable lately. At first, the dizziness had frightened her a little, but nothing was more horrifying than being yelled at by Mr. Ackerman for being the slowest runner. When he yelled, all the boys laughed and pointed at her, and the dizziness would turn to nausea. Just because she knew to expect the reaction didn't mean she was comfortable with it, no matter how often she'd experienced it.

Reluctantly, she followed her classmates out of the locker room. They threw open the door to the gym and Mr. Ackerman stood there, whistle in hand, yelling at the boys who were already running. "Get going! I don't want to see any laziness out there!"

He spotted the girls and continued his tirade. "Girls, get going! Where have you been?" He stuck the whistle in his mouth and the shrill *thweeeeet* pierced her eardrums. Brianna began running with her friends. She burst into a sprint, vowing not to be the last one today. She couldn't tolerate that humiliation for another day. The boys already finished their run and began shooting some baskets. The too-familiar ringing in her ears had dizziness and nausea following on its heels.

No, damn it. I will not be last today. She pushed through the dizziness and attempted to maintain her pace. She felt some of the other girls behind her. Her pace slowed. *No, oh no.* She pushed a little harder and suddenly everything went dark. She lost control and stumbled forward as her legs gave way. Sneakers squeaked and basketballs bounced through Brianna's brain, fading as she fell unconscious to the highly polished gymnasium floor.

***

The phone rang for the fourth time in ten minutes. *Give it a rest.* Amy listened to her sister leave yet another message. *I am a grown woman who doesn't need to be constantly babysat.*

"Amy, I know you can hear me. You're the only person under ninety who still has an answering machine. Please just pick up the phone. You know what? If you don't answer, I guess I'll just have to drive out there and make you talk to me."

Amy lifted her head from her kitchen table and contemplated picking up the phone, just to ensure that her sister didn't come over today, but she couldn't summon enough energy to stand up. Instead, she laid her head back on the table. Her greasy, unwashed hair fell out of the loosely-placed bun on top of her head and sprawled out like a fan.

"That's it, Amy. I'm coming over. I'll be there in twenty minutes. You have to eat something. I'm really worried." The answering machine beeped, signaling that Nancy had hung up. Amy figured she was probably already on her way.

Amy looked down at the bathrobe that hung from her narrow frame. She had been wearing it since last week, when Nancy had forced her to take a shower. *Great, she's probably going to make me take another shower, and worse, she's going to make me eat something.* The very thought of food made Amy gag. Last week, Nancy had brought over a bag of microwavable foods for Amy's convenience. She was going to be alarmed to find the food had gone uneaten. Yesterday, Amy managed to choke down some dry toast with her coffee, but mostly she'd been living on coffee and apple juice. She really couldn't stomach anything else.

Honestly, she couldn't stomach much of anything these days, and her sister was at the top of that list. She knew Nancy meant well, but she couldn't possibly understand her state of mind, and Amy resented her for that. She also knew she couldn't expect her sister to understand since Amy certainly wouldn't talk about it. Their mother had taught them long ago that a lady never discussed her feelings.

Twenty minutes later, like clockwork, with Amy's head still on the table, Nancy and their mother Claire burst through the front door, arms loaded with groceries. "Amy, I swear to God, is it so much to ask you to pick up your phone? I'm worried sick about you. Please just give me that much. Just answer the phone," Nancy exclaimed.

Amy picked her head up from the table for the second time today. "I tried."

Nancy looked exasperated as she put the groceries away. She stopped suddenly, examining the contents of the cupboards. "The food I brought you last week is still here? You haven't eaten anything in a whole week? Amy, you're going to make yourself sick."

"I had some toast." Amy laid her head back on the table.

Claire rolled her eyes and took over putting the groceries away.

"I can see that your hygiene hasn't improved." Nancy sat next to her sister. "Can I please make you some eggs or something? Will you please eat something? Anything you want. You name it. I'll be so happy to make it for you. Please?"

Amy stared at her sister. She didn't remember her always being this irritating. *When had she become so annoying? She used to be such a sweet little sister.* In fact, the old Nancy had never really paid much attention to her at all, let alone the doting and carrying on that had somehow become the new Nancy. She was always too wrapped up in her own life and too consumed with work to include Amy in anything. In the past, Amy would've loved to finally spend some time with the sister she barely knew. Now, Nancy was a little gnat that couldn't be shooed away. *Why won't she just leave me alone?*

Nancy sighed and stared back. "How about some tea, can I make you some tea?"

Amy thought about it for a minute. If it would mean that Nancy would leave her alone again for the next week, she could manage to drink some tea. She nodded almost imperceptibly.

Nancy victoriously jumped from her seat at the table and filled the teapot with water. They sat silently for a while as they waited for the water to boil. Claire was still busy putting the groceries away, conspicuous with her silence. The phone rang again, and Amy shot her sister a dirty look.

"Don't look at me." Nancy gave her a wry smile.

"Amy, please talk to me." The sound of Luke's voice sucked all of the oxygen from Amy's lungs. "This has been so hard for me too, and I need you. I miss you so much." His voice broke as he choked on a sob and hung up the phone.

Nancy watched Amy's face, but it didn't change at all. It was as though she hadn't even heard him. She didn't bother to ask if Amy had spoken to her husband at all in the last week. Luke's message had made it pretty clear that Amy still wasn't talking to him. The teapot began to sing, and Nancy brushed away a tear. Things were obviously getting worse, and she was at the end of her rope. Out of ideas. She couldn't force Amy to get help, but neither could she stand by and watch her sister slowly kill herself with personal neglect.

She poured three cups of tea and set one in front of Amy. She tried to consider this day a positive one. She actually had been able to convince her sister to drink something other than apple juice. Would it be pushing it to run a bath for her? Nancy decided it wasn't worth riling Amy by asking. Tomorrow was another day.

"Amy, get up this instant." Claire spoke for the first time since their arrival, her lips tightly pursed.

"No," Amy petulantly replied.

Claire nudged Nancy. "You need to get her up."

"I'm not getting up. I didn't ask you to come here. Get out of here. Both of you." Amy was seething, her eyes flashing surprising fire.

Claire huffed out a disgusted sigh before walking out of the house, slamming the front door behind her. Nancy stood staring at Amy for a moment longer. "Call me if you need anything."

Amy just grunted.

***

Her eyes fluttered open and she could barely make out the blurred faces around her. Mr. Ackerman's voice, asking her if she was alright, was strangely hollow. "Julia, call the nurse," he yelled out as he was checking Brianna's pulse. Brianna attempted to sit up, but the dizziness overcame her again. She lay back down and closed her eyes.

"Brianna, honey, I need you to open your eyes. Can you open your eyes, honey?" Brianna opened her eyes again and found the school nurse, Ms. Harrison, studying her. She glanced around and became acutely aware of thirty-five seventh graders staring down at her. She groaned inwardly. *This couldn't possibly get any worse.* Unfortunately, she was starting to feel better and it was making room for the waves of humiliation that were washing over her.

"Can you sit up?" Ms. Harrison put her hand on Brianna's back, gently assisting her. Brianna sat up, still slouching against one arm, and rubbed her head. All the boys in the class began to applaud. She spotted Mark in the crowd and could feel tears welling up in her eyes.

Brianna looked pleadingly at Ms. Harrison. "Can we get out of here?"

"Sure, honey." Ms. Harrison offered her a hand and together they walked to her office.

Brianna cringed. She was going to have to go to another school after the spectacle she made of herself today. The nurse, seeming to sense her humiliation, leaned into Brianna and said, "You know honey, the only reason the boys act like that is because they have a crush on you."

Brianna swallowed her embarrassment and managed to smile politely at her. She did her best to ignore the nurse's awkwardness for the rest of the way to her office. When they arrived, Ms. Harrison directed her toward the cot in the corner. "Sit down here, honey; I'm going to call your parents."

"It's just me and my dad."

Ms. Harrison paused, "Alright, I'll call your dad."

Brianna nodded listlessly. *Good luck getting a hold of him*. She held her breath as the events that happened just moments before came rushing back. It was worse than she'd even thought it would be. She would rather be the slowest girl in the class than the one who passed out. She slumped down on the bed. And of course the whole thing had to happen right in front of Mark.

Ms. Harrison reappeared. "I couldn't reach your dad. I talked to someone at his work, but he said he was unavailable to talk. I told him it was urgent and he still seemed to think that he was unavailable. Until we hear from your dad, I'm afraid you're just going to have to wait right here and rest. I'm going to have to keep an eye on you. Fainting can be a pretty serious thing. You're lucky you didn't hurt yourself when you hit the floor."

Brianna nodded again and lay back on the bed. She didn't mind having to stay in the nurse's office. She wouldn't mind if she had to stay there forever. She was never going to live down this humiliation.

And two hours later, when the final bell rang, they still hadn't heard from her dad.

"Can I go home now?" Brianna stood up from the cot.

Ms. Harrison shrugged, unsure of what more she could do. "I guess so. Please have your dad take you to the doctor."

Brianna waited until the halls sounded quiet before she left.

***

Jack's eyes slowly opened. He groggily gazed around the doctor's lounge and realized he must have dozed off. Still half asleep, he glanced at his phone to check his schedule and remembered he didn't have any more surgeries scheduled for today. A long exhale that ended with a barely audible sigh signified his relief. The only thing he wanted to do was to get home and relax. He rubbed a tender spot on his lower back before struggling a bit to get off the couch. He wasn't quite as spry as he once was. The last ten years of his medical career as a cardiac electro physiologist at the university hospital had been rewarding, not to mention lucrative, but lately those rewards were replaced with fatigue and boredom. It didn't help that he could practically perform catheter ablations in his sleep. His compulsive need to succeed, coupled with his competitive drive, whispered to him that the status quo wasn't working.

The passing of ten years marked a new record for him. His position at the university had held his attention far longer than he had ever dreamed it would. It was probably mostly due to the ever-changing technology and the life-saving innovations he witnessed on an almost daily basis relating to the study and treatment of the heart rhythms. However, even that failed to interest him anymore. That old familiar feeling of boredom and ennui dragged on his soul. It crept up on him in its usual way. The boredom suffocated him, and he longed for freedom.

"Dr. Parker?" He turned towards the door when he heard his name and saw a nurse, whose name he could never remember. "The patient's family would like to thank you."

Rather than feeling pride from another successful procedure, Jack felt irritated. "Can you please talk to them for me? I'm in a real hurry."

Before the nurse could respond, he brushed past her and walked out. Soon, he was on his way, with his foot to the floor in his brand-new Ferrari. An impulse buy last week that he hoped would tamp down his anxious feelings long enough for him to decide just what to do next with his life. He thought the car would distract him, but it dawned on him that the car was a poor salve. The closer the calendar crept toward Melissa's birthday, the more intense his feelings became. Just like every year before.

He leaned toward the steering wheel and rubbed his back again. The dull back pain had persisted for months now, maybe more, but it seemed to be getting worse. He tried not to think about his age. As he turned his car into his winding driveway, his mind meandered to a bottle of Glenrothes, a Cohiba, and the baseball game. He could practically taste the scotch as he pulled up to his sprawling home that took up over 10,000 square feet of his six-acre patch of lush and manicured foliage.

His heart sank when he saw her car in the driveway. *Did we have a date tonight? Had I forgotten?* He was definitely not in the mood for her tonight. It wasn't that he didn't care about her. In fact, in all of his 61 years, he'd never cared so much for anyone as he did for her, and that seemed to be the problem. He didn't particularly like that he cared so much. For the most part, he preferred to be alone.

He pulled his car into the garage and braced himself as he opened the door to his home.

"Hi, honey," she called from somewhere inside the house. "How's the new ride?"

He flipped his keys onto the table by the door. "She's pretty sweet," he muttered unenthusiastically. Suddenly, she materialized, looking radiant in a low-cut dress and a martini in each hand. Her green eyes sparkled as she stretched out a long smooth arm to hand him his drink.

"Well hello to you, too." Jack appreciatively accepted the drink.

"Hungry?" She took a sip of her martini. "I told Mary to take the night off."

"Don't tell me you cooked!" Jack looked at her incredulously.

Amanda flipped her hair and swiped at his arm in a mock punch as she giggled at his hilarious statement. "Oh honey, you're so funny." She tucked her hand into the fold of his elbow and led him into the kitchen. "I meant it would be nice to go out to eat instead of having Mary cook us something here. I haven't seen you in a few days, and I've missed you so much."

"Let's go sit in the drawing room instead. It's more comfortable in there." Jack thought about his aching back as he redirected them into another room toward an oversized leather couch that sat atop a marble floor.

"I love that you call it a drawing room. It sounds so old-fashioned and exotic." Amanda smiled at him as she eased herself down next to him on the couch and crossed her legs at the ankles.

He smirked a little to himself at Amanda's comment. Old habits certainly died hard. So much of his mother was still alive in him.

"Why don't we spend more time in here? This is such a pretty room." She looked over at the piano. "Play something for me."

Inspired by her suggestion, Jack stood up and walked to the piano. He played a tune with one hand while holding his martini in the other. He hadn't played seriously for years. *Do I still know how?* He had been classically trained on the piano, and had been quite good, once upon a time.

People used to tell him he had a gift, and he had loved to play more than anything else. Eventually, medical school and his career consumed all of his time, and for a while, he only dabbled a bit during a social occasion here or there. Jack eventually stopped doing that, too, and now he couldn't remember a time that he'd played.

"Why did they call it a drawing room anyway? Did they draw things in it? Did they have drawing tables and easels and things?" Amanda had a serious look of confusion on her face. She walked over to where he still stood by the piano.

He ruffled her hair a little and kissed her smooth cheek. "I think it was originally called a withdrawing room. From what they were withdrawing I'm not really sure. Eventually, I think it came to be known as the drawing room because it was a place where you could draw all of your guests together."

"Maybe they were withdrawing from their girlfriends because they were tired of dodging questions about marriage." Amanda crossed her arms across her body, her lips formed a pout that wasn't exactly childish but neither was it pretty. She wasn't wasting any time tonight. Usually it wasn't until well into dessert, and his second or third glass of scotch, before she started pressing marriage.

Amanda became more and more insistent, pushing the benefits of marriage, but he really wasn't sure it was what he wanted. He wasn't sure that it *wasn't* what he wanted either, so in the meantime, he just kept stalling, knowing he was stringing her along. What else could he do? He didn't want to marry her, at least not now, but he didn't want to lose her either. He hadn't figured out a good solution to this problem yet, and he certainly wasn't prepared to start dodging these bullets so early in the evening.

"Why do you think I picked this room?" Jack winked at her hoping that humor would buy him some time.

With all the charm of a buzz saw, Amanda stomped out of the room. Jack drained his martini and rubbed his back. He groaned as he went after her. This was going to be a very long night.

***

After throwing her mother and sister out, Amy dragged herself over to the front door and angrily turned the deadbolt shut to ensure that they would not enter her home again. Claire and Nancy remained on the front porch of Amy's brownstone, and she was able to overhear what her mother said.

"Amy needs to pull herself out of this funk that she's in. Go buy herself a new outfit, get a pedicure, or have an ice cream sundae. If she'd just get back out in the world, she'd see that she is fine." Claire stamped her foot petulantly.

Amy threw open the front door. "I can hear you!" she screamed, and slammed the door in their stunned faces. She picked up her teacup and jettisoned it against the door. The china smashed into antagonistic shards. *Why can't everyone just leave me alone?* The pain was most excruciating when she was being forced to pretend that she wasn't in pain. Screw them. She didn't have to talk to any of them. *A milkshake isn't going to make this better. What is wrong with them?* They were acting as if she had a splinter in her finger and just needed to have her tears kissed away. Her sister, her husband, her mother—they could all go to hell. She could sit in her bathrobe until the end of time if she wanted to and no one could stop her. She picked up a picture frame with her husband's smiling face in it and hurled that against the door too. The glass shattered and mingled with the china.

It wasn't long before she fully lost control of the rage that boiled inside of her. Amy blindly made her way to the living room and grabbed a bottle of vodka. In one fluid motion, she cracked off the cap and flipped it into the trash. She walked to the kitchen and took a pint glass out of the cupboard, filling it halfway. She found the orange juice that Nancy left and filled the rest of the glass up. That was it. She'd had it.

Nancy had suggested last week that maybe she start going to church again. Amy seethed and contemplated killing her sister for suggesting it. God couldn't possibly exist. And if he did, she didn't like him anyway. She didn't want anything to do with him. Any God that could take a fifteen-year-old child from his mother was no God of hers. He could go to hell with the rest of them.

She finished her drink and subtly swayed one way, catching herself as she made another drink. How could Luke just call her and act like everything should be fine, when he was the one responsible for Jonathan's death? How was it possible that he was confused about why their marriage was falling apart? She was so confounded and angry that everyone expected her to carry on and put her marriage back together. The hatred in her heart for Luke consumed her, and she was certain she would never forgive him. It was unconscionable what he did, and unless he could give her Jonathan back, he could forget about her ever talking to him again, much less fixing their marriage.

She slammed back her second drink and lay down on the couch. Her head was spinning and she was starting to get a little bit of a headache. Good; it was a relief to have a different kind of pain. The alcohol clouded her mind and she got lost in thoughts of Jonathan. She remembered the first time she looked into his eyes when he was born; she remembered his first day of kindergarten; she remembered when he was old enough to ride his bike on his own; she remembered when she tucked him into bed at night; she remembered teaching him how to drive. She remembered his first seizure and the fear of helplessness. That day marked the beginning of the end. *What good is life if I don't have my son?* She'd looked in all directions and couldn't find comfort anywhere. She felt the hope of ever feeling at peace again effortlessly slip out of her life.

She began to scream. She screamed until her lungs hurt; she screamed until her throat bled; she screamed until no sound at all would come out. Then she screamed some more.

Chapter 2

Amanda laid her head on the arm of her couch. He said he would call tonight, but so far, he hadn't. That wasn't unusual behavior for him, but that Amanda was putting up with it? That was truly astonishing. Before she met Jack, she never would've dreamed of letting a man string her along. Just a few weeks ago, he'd actually stood her up. She protectively pulled a blanket around her at the memory of it. He promised to meet her at their usual place for dinner, and he hadn't even bothered to show up. Later, when she called him on it, he claimed that it had slipped his mind. She didn't know what was worse, forgetting all about her or purposefully not showing up? Her lip quivered for a moment as she thought of it. Either way, it wasn't good.

What has gotten into me? I need to kick him to the curb, so why aren't I? Why can't I shake him? I've always been in control of my relationships. I dictate the terms. I've broken up with men for lessor things than this. She knew that a girl as desirable as she could have any available man that she wanted. This always surprised her, but it didn't stop her from becoming accustomed to it.

Still, there was a side of Jack that kept her with him – even if that side rarely saw daylight.

She saw the softer Jack. She doubted that many people had ever seen it. That version of Jack had appeared so rarely, that now, as she sat waiting for a phone call that might never come, she wondered if she had imagined those times. Admittedly, no one would accuse him of being the romantic type. There were never the gestures, neither grand nor small, and perish the thought of him ever surprising her with anything. But there were times when he would let her in, let her see some of his vulnerabilities. At least that's what she thought.

But lately, there had been so many mixed signals that stoked her insecurities. Maybe she really had never seen any side of him except the arrogant, self-centered asshole who apparently lost her number. *Why does he get to dictate the terms of our relationship? Everything is always on his time, even his so-called vulnerabilities.*

I wish I didn't love him. I wish I could take it all back.

As she willed herself to forget about him, her cell phone rang. She smirked, and the pessimism faded. Typical Jack. He had an uncanny ability to place well-timed phone calls. Of course she would forgive him.

"I thought for a minute that you weren't going to call." Amanda cringed at how desperate that sounded.

Jack didn't waste any time. "I'm starving. Pick you up in twenty minutes?"

Giddy, she bounced off the couch and quickly got herself ready for dinner, forgetting the despondent feelings of just five minutes ago.

While the restaurant bustled about her, Amanda's good feelings began to fade again. Even though Jack had taken her out, the "date" felt like her own monologue. Jack was never one to be particularly warm or conversational, but in the four years they had been together she never knew him to be this distant. She studied Jack intently and watched him quietly shovel his food into his mouth, barely looking up. She wasn't quite sure exactly when it happened, but at some point, Jack changed. He didn't hear her when she talked, or worse, he ignored her. He seemed annoyed or irritated whenever she called and always had an excuse to get off the phone. Jack barely noticed her appearance anymore. He used to not be able to keep his hands off of her, but that changed too. Tonight, she was trying to give him the benefit of the doubt. She knew it was his sister's birthday, which had always been a hard day for him. But still, his bullshit was wearing thin.

As the clinking of silverware filled in for their conversation, she continued to wonder why she felt stuck here. Her push for marriage intensified. She knew that he avoided the topic, but on the other hand, she could sense that some part of him really did want to marry her. If she was honest with herself, she could have seen this conflict coming a long time ago. Since they met four years ago, he had celebrated his 60th birthday, and she had celebrated her 30th. Amanda's friends and family warned her about getting involved with such an older man, but despite these warnings, she fell in love with him anyway. Amanda knew that a 61-year-old lifelong childless bachelor might not race to the altar or register for a stroller, but her wishful thinking got in the way of her common sense.

A crash coming from the kitchen interrupted her reverie but not the reality of her situation. She found herself right in the spot her friends had warned her about, a 31-year-old woman who invested the last four years of her life with a man who didn't want to marry her. She let her eyes flicker over the empty spot on her left ring finger. At this moment, he couldn't even seem to be bothered to give her the time of day, much less a baby. They had been sitting at dinner for thirty minutes, and he'd barely spoken a word. He busily glanced around the restaurant at God knows what.

"Jack?"

He stuck his fork in his mouth and grunted. "Mmmm?"

"I asked you how your food is." Amanda set her fork down.

Jack pushed his chair back and got up from the table. "It's fine, honey. Excuse me; I need to use the restroom."

Amanda stared at his back as he walked away. She shook her head and poured herself another glass of wine as she sat with the echo of her desperation. She tried to blink away the tears that were welling up behind her eyelids. One tear escaped and as she quickly swept it into her napkin, she cleared her throat. *It's going to be okay. This is not as bad as it seems. It's just because it's Melissa's birthday, that's all. Don't make this about you.*

Jack returned to the table and sat awkwardly in his seat.

"You okay?" Amanda noticed he looked uncomfortable. His face seemed pinched.

"Yes, I'm fine. My back seems to be hurting a little. I'm sure it's okay; maybe I just need to rest. Are you done eating?" Jack pushed his chair back again, flipping a few large bills from his pocket onto the table without another word.

Amanda stared at her now-full glass of wine and sighed. "Sure, honey. If you're not feeling well, we should go."

"Come on; I'll take you home." Jack put his hand on the small of her back and led her out of the restaurant.

Jack knew how irritated Amanda had been when he dropped her off, but tonight more pressing things were on his mind. He figured he could always make it up to her later. He swerved his Ferrari into a grocery store parking lot and, once he was inside, selected three colorful helium balloons. As he had every year on her birthday for the last forty-three years, he drove for an hour to his sister's favorite spot, an old stone bridge that arched over a creek. They spent a lot of time there as kids. The bridge was connected to a footpath that burrowed deep into the woods. They knew that pathway with their eyes closed, having spent many hours running and hiding in the woods and swimming and floating in the creek. But mostly, they passed their time on the bridge. And so, every year he came back here to where they always loved to play as children.

As he stood on the bridge, he looked up into the heavens and let the balloons go. "Happy birthday, Melissa."

He stood gazing upward as he watched the balloons float up into the sky. Somehow it made him feel better to offer his sister the balloons on her birthday, even though he knew the balloons would probably only end up stuck in a tree somewhere.

As he stood on the bridge, memories of their childhood escapades flooded his mind. Sometimes they would go to fish, or throw pennies in after their wishes. Sometimes they would go to hide from their mother when she was particularly angry or in a bad mood. Other times, they would go just to catch up with each other or to share secrets. After Father died, nothing had ever been the same. No one could protect them now from their unpredictable mother. The bridge had been their haven. It provided them a much-needed refuge. They imagined that bridge could take them just about anywhere, and it really didn't matter, as long as it went anywhere but home.

As he now felt the old stone beneath him and stared at the water below, he thought for just a moment that he could feel Melissa there with him. He pressed his thumbs into his eyes to stop the tears that he knew would eventually escape. He shuffled to one end of the bridge and went right to the place where she had once painted her initials with nail polish. The weather had, long ago, washed the initials away, but this time Jack remembered to bring a bottle of nail polish. He slowly and meticulously painted her initials onto the exact spot where her hand had painted them decades earlier.

As he looked at the neatly written letters, he smiled as he remembered her. He took his shoes and socks off and sat down on the bridge, letting his bare feet dangle over the side, above the creek. It wasn't long before the tears overtook him.

"Please forgive me, Melissa. Please forgive me. I'm lost. I don't know what to do. I'm so alone here without you." Jack sobbed into his hands, a futile effort to wash the blood of his sister from them. Being on their bridge caused a deluge of haunting memories, but being away from their spot caused an unyielding loneliness.

Hours passed, and he couldn't bring himself to leave. As every time he came to visit Melissa here, he always found it difficult to go. It was as though he abandoned her all over again. He was unable to protect her in life, and this bridge served as a crushing reminder. Although his tears had dried an hour ago, he knew the misery would live on in his heart.

He forced himself to his feet, choked out a farewell to Melissa and waved. "See you next year, sis." He turned with his head hanging down and left the way he had come.

***

After a particularly grueling day at work, Jack limped into his home and went straight for the kitchen. His back ached during all of his surgeries today and he couldn't wait to lie down. He poked through a cupboard, looking for something to help his pain.

"Hello, Mr. Parker." Mary was busy cleaning the kitchen. "How was your day?"

Jack grunted. "Not good."

He spotted ibuprofen in the cupboard and popped a few. Maybe it would help eliminate his blinding pain. It had been going on for so long it started to affect his mood. These days, his mood wasn't all that great to being with.

Mary eyed the pain relievers. "Not feeling well?"

"Not really. You can go home. I'm just going to relax."

"I'll finish up here and be on my way." Mary continued to wipe down the countertop.

Jack hobbled into the living room and poured himself a glass of scotch. As he laid himself down on the couch, he grabbed the remote and flipped on the television. The weather man rambled on about how unseasonably cold things were going to get.

He found a comfortable enough position when his phone rang. He reached into his pocket and saw that it was Amanda. He sighed and forwarded the call to voicemail. His pain wouldn't allow him to deal with her tonight. She'd want to go out, and he just wasn't feeling up to it. He would call her tomorrow; she would understand.

Amanda listened as Jack's phone went directly to voicemail. This was the sixth time in a row, just this week, that he had done that. It was time to read the writing on the wall. The fact that he didn't answer - again - made a clear statement. He was over her. If he wanted to continue a relationship with her, he had a funny way of showing it. And if he didn't want to be with her, it only meant that he didn't have the guts to tell her. She deserved better. It broke her heart to think that she cared so much and to him she had meant so little that he could just pretend that she didn't exist when she called him. *How had I ever convinced myself that he had actually loved me? How could I have been so wrong?*

She resisted an urge to call her friend Adrienne. Last week, she and Adrienne sat on this very couch and argued about moving on.

"*Amanda, you have to see what's going on here.*" *Adrienne was adamant about the way she felt Jack had been treating her friend.* "*He is never going to commit to you. He never committed to anyone. Why should this be any different for him? This has been going on long enough for you to see that. Please, honey, I wouldn't say this if I didn't really just know that it's true. When are you going to let him go?*"

"*It's not that easy.*" *Amanda wept into her hands.*

Adrienne reached out to touch her arm. "*I know it's not, but it's not going to be easy to stay with him either. You two are driving each other crazy because you are not on the same page. You're not aligned with each other.*"

Amanda wiped away her tears with the back of her hand. "*I guess deep down I always knew this day would come, but I wasn't prepared for how hard it would be.*"

Adrienne was silent for a few moments and then added, "*You know, there's always my friend Derek.*"

Amanda glared at her.

"*Okay, okay. Maybe it's too soon to mention him again, but I really need to let you know that he's a possibility for you. He's a great guy, and if you don't snag him, believe me, it won't be long until some other lucky girl does.*"

Amanda had always been confident that Jack was the one for her. Even if they agreed to never have children, she had always believed in her heart he would at least marry her. Now she watched that possibility slip further and further away. He wouldn't even pick up the phone when she called. *How can he do this to me? How can he be so insensitive?* She felt her blood pressure begin to rise.

Vengefully, she picked up her phone. *Why not?* She'd call Adrienne. It was time to admit that her friend was right.

Within twenty minutes, Amanda agreed to come out with Adrienne and some friends to meet Derek. Amanda looked around her closet and decided on a miniskirt. For four years she had closed herself off to other possibilities, but tonight wasn't going to be one of those nights. Her friends had been right. Jack was a bad idea from the beginning. Her hands trembled as she slipped her feet into a pair of Manolos. She and Jack would never be on the same page, and she didn't have any more time to lose. She wasn't getting any younger.

She tapped her foot nervously as she waited for a cab. She already changed her mind three times and had even considered calling Adrienne to tell her she wasn't coming, but she knew it was too late. Adrienne already told Derek she was coming, and Jack hadn't called her back. Besides, what was the big deal? It wasn't as though she was cheating on Jack. She hadn't even met Derek yet.

Still, Amanda couldn't help feeling that what she was doing was wrong. But was it? She asked herself as she looked out into the city street and saw a taxi approaching. Was it any worse than what Jack was doing? Maybe it was high time he got a dose of his own medicine. She threw her hand in the air to hail the cab.

Amanda opened the back door of the taxi. "28th and 3rd."

***

Brianna unlocked the door to the apartment she shared with her dad. She threw her backpack on the floor and headed for the kitchen. Dismissed from gym class until she had a doctor's note clearing her to participate had lifted a huge weight off of her shoulders. She physically felt better, and getting out of gym was the icing on the cake. She knew it would be a long time before her dad found time, let alone money, to get her a check-up. She felt pretty confident that her break from gym was going to be indefinite. More importantly though, she was super excited because Erin told her that Julia told her that Rob told her that Mark told him that Mark liked Brianna.

Julia and Erin had tracked her down in the cafeteria to give her the good news. Julia slammed her tray down next to Brianna's, as Brianna slid over to make room for her to sit down.

"Okay, Erin, tell her," Julia demanded with a smile on her face.

Erin slid into the seat across from them. "Okay, are you ready for this?" Erin paused dramatically. "Mark likes you. He wants to come to the movies with us this weekend."

Brianna choked on her chocolate milk.

Julia pounded her on the back. "Are you okay? Did you hear what Erin just said?"

Brianna nodded and the three of them squealed with delight. She had liked Mark for so long, but never in a million years did she think he would like her back. This was unbelievable news and the three of them giggled throughout their entire lunch hour.

"I can't believe he likes me." Brianna bit her lip, and quickly added, "But I might not be able to go to the movies this weekend. My dad and I are probably traveling to California." She took another sip of her milk and looked at Erin. "I'll find out."

Erin glanced knowingly at her and Brianna quickly averted her eyes.

Now alone in her sparsely furnished apartment, reality sank in. She realized, of course, that not only were they not really going to California that weekend, or ever, but also that her dad would never let her go to the movies with her friends. She stifled the thought as she looked for something to eat. She pulled open the refrigerator, not expecting to find much. It was usually her job to walk to the grocery store and shop, while her dad worked on Saturdays, but she hadn't been able to go last week because Dad used the grocery money to pay the rent. Much to her surprise, she found a gallon of milk. *Hmm, Dad must have stopped on his way home last night.* That would explain why she hadn't seen him before she went to bed. She pulled the milk from the fridge and found some cereal in the cabinet. Dinner tonight would be a luxury. Too bad her dad couldn't be here to share it with her. That's when she heard the key in the lock, and she jumped up in excitement.

"Dad!" Brianna ran and threw her arms around him as he walked through the doorway.

Lawrence belly-laughed and scooped her up in his arms. "I missed you, too. I'm sorry I didn't get to tuck you in last night, baby, but I did give you a kiss while you were sleeping."

"I know, Dad. You always do." Brianna grabbed him a bowl from the cupboard. Too excited to see her dad, she figured she would wait to ask him until later about the movies. Right now, Mark didn't matter; she just wanted to spend some much-needed time with her dad.

Lawrence squeezed Brianna's arm and gave her a smile as they sat down together with their bowls of cereal.

"How are you feeling? Have you been feeling dizzy or anything again lately?" Lawrence set his spoon down and look at her with concern.

"Oh, I'm fine, Dad. I feel great. Especially because I don't have to run in gym class anymore."

He nodded and picked up his spoon again. "And how are Erin and Julia? I suppose there is some federal emergency that they're dealing with?"

He winked at Brianna, and she laughed.

Lawrence shoveled the rest of his cereal into his mouth and stood up from the table. "I have to go back to work, baby. That was just a short break."

"It's okay, Dad. I know." She hugged him goodbye with a heavy heart, and with a sad smile, she wandered over to her room.

She threw herself down on the bed and felt tears flood her eyes as she thought about her predicament. At school she had the opportunity to delude herself that Mark's sudden interest was actually a good thing. Now she realized she had been kidding herself. She knew she wouldn't be able to go the movies. There was no way that her dad was going to give her the money to go. Even if he had it, which she was sure he didn't, he would never let her spend it on something as frivolous as a movie. She wouldn't dare ask her friends for money; that was way too embarrassing. Even Erin, who was her most trusted friend, didn't know the gravity of their financial problems, even though she knew a little bit about it. She preferred her friends to think that she and her dad traveled to fun places every weekend. It gave her friends the idea that Brianna and her dad had a lot of money and led very exciting lives, but it also served the purpose of not having to explain to her friends the real reason why she could never go out with them on the weekends.

        To make matters worse, even if by some miracle her dad was able to scrounge up enough money for the movie, what would she wear anyway? She didn't even bother to look in her closet. It held little more than bare hangers. She'd outgrown most of her clothes from the year before, and replenishing her wardrobe was low on the financial priority list. The last time her dad gave her a few dollars for clothes, she bought a new top from a thrift store and hoped no one would notice that she wore the same two pair of jeans to school every week.

She would never be like the other kids. None of them were rich necessarily, but they always seemed to have enough. They certainly had enough to go to the movies on the weekends. Brianna always felt like a loser around them - like she never fully fit in. Insecurely, she spent hours in the morning curling her hair just to straighten it again, and finally deciding on curls again, only to leave for school with a ponytail.

Brianna never felt confident that the other kids would accept her. They always liked her, but she felt like she worked harder than the other kids to fit in and certainly worked harder to hide how poor she was. She wandered into the bathroom and glumly gazed at herself in the mirror. She filled a cup with water from the sink and took a slow sip. She spit the water back at her reflection in the mirror. Disgusted with both herself and her stupid life, she slammed the bathroom door and headed back to her bedroom.

She hated herself, and she hated her life. *Why do I have to be different from everyone else? Why can't Dad just be like everyone else's dads?* The other dads only had one job that they went to every day, and they managed to have dinner with their kids and extra spending money for them. Her dad had two - and sometimes even three - jobs at once and could barely pay rent. *Why couldn't he figure it out? Maybe if Mom was here things would be better.*

As the thought crossed her mind, red shame splashed her cheeks. Her dad went to his crappy jobs every day to give her the best possible life under the circumstances. She blinked quickly as her eyes brimmed with tears and turned her radio up as loud as it would go. She tried to get her mind back on the fact that Mark liked her. It just wasn't fair. *So what if Mark likes me? I can't hide the fact that I'm poor for very long, and when he finds out, he'll hate me for sure.* Tension built inside of her, suffocated by the circumstance. She was utterly miserable in her life but unable to mutter a complaint. She raged back into the bathroom and hunted in the cupboard until she found a razor. She pulled off her pants and sat down on the tiled floor. She pressed the blade into her thigh, just enough to make it bleed.

Chapter 3

Jack hobbled through the door and went straight to the kitchen, hoping to find a hot meal waiting for him. His back was getting worse, and ibuprofen was no longer managing the pain. He'd taken some muscle relaxants just before he left the hospital, but he knew they wouldn't sit well for long in his empty stomach. Looking around the vacant kitchen, he vaguely remembered Mary asking him for the night off, for a birthday party, or something. He hadn't really been listening when she asked. Annoyed now, he hurriedly poured himself a bowl of cereal and scarfed it down.

Before long he assumed his usual prone position on the couch. As he lay watching the news, his thoughts drifted to Amanda. *I wonder how she's doing?* Perhaps he missed her a little. He'd lost track of how long it had been since they'd seen each other, or even talked, but he thought at least a week had passed. He imagined her irritation and knew he would somehow have to make it up to her. He picked up his phone and called her. She didn't answer, surprisingly; she was practically married to her phone. He let his gaze drift back to the television and felt his eyelids getting heavy.

Forty minutes later, he woke up to a growling stomach. Perhaps going out for dinner was a good idea, but he didn't want to go by himself. He checked his phone, but it was radio silence from Amanda. He tried to call her again, but as before, she didn't answer. *Where was she?*

Despite his limp, he stomped into the kitchen and looked around. *What to eat, what to eat?* He stared at the box of cereal he left out on the counter and hesitated, but he knew he had no energy to cook. A memory flitted through his brain of his mother's annoyance with cereal.

"For heaven's sake, Jack, cereal is not a proper food. Have Isadora fix you something." He could still see his mother's sneer. Isadora would then wink at him and whip up something that she knew he would like that would also please Mrs. Parker.

He smiled as he defiantly poured some cereal into a bowl and remembered. Isadora represented everything that his mother didn't. She was loving and compassionate, nurturing and supportive. Jack couldn't remember a time when Isadora wasn't there for him. She worked for his mother a long time, even before he and his sister were born. She was a family member as far as he and Melissa were concerned.

As he crunched the cereal, he wondered what had ever happened to Isadora. After he'd left home for Yale, he hadn't come back much. The house didn't feel like home, especially after Melissa died. One Christmas morning, many years later, he called his mother, who told him that Isadora had left. Jack never bothered to find out why. He'd been too busy trying to start his new career to be bothered with the past. It seemed that nowhere was far enough away. Even back then, he had been sprinting toward the future, never looking back. He didn't care to reflect on his relationship with Isadora because he didn't have time. Demands of his medical career conveniently suffocated any lingering feelings or emotions. But deep down, he knew that it was too painful to look back. He was too weak of a man to face the pain.

He smiled now though as he remembered her and poured himself another bowl. He and Isadora were always close when he was growing up. When he skinned his knees as a little child, she scooped him into her arms to kiss the pain away. When he was sleepy, she would tuck him in with a bedtime story. When he brought six of his ravenous friends home after school, she would prepare them a feast. When he lost the lacrosse championship in high school, she saw him through the heart-breaking disappointment.

They even had their own way of communicating. When Mother had guests over for dinner, which happened quite a lot, the evening had the usual tone and posture of self-righteousness. He and Isadora would tolerate the pompousness by exchanging subtle eye rolls and raised eyebrows.

He dumped his empty bowl into the sink. Isadora knew too much about him, which was a problem. Strangers provided an odd comfort because they didn't know anything about him. He could be whomever he wanted with strangers. His friends knew too much and only served to remind him of everything that he was that he couldn't accept.

As a result, he never made real connections or bonds with anyone. He lost touch with his high school friends when he went to college, and he drifted away from his college friends when he went to medical school.

Now, as he pathetically shuffled back to the couch, it saddened him that he never really said goodbye to Isadora. He offered a silent apology to her and poured himself a glass of scotch. Reaching into his pocket, he pulled out his phone. *Have I missed a call from Amanda?* No new calls showed on the screen. Grumbling, he tried to get comfortable on the couch. At least the muscle relaxants were helping; maybe he'd actually get some sleep tonight.

***

Did Dad lose one of his jobs? Brianna had to wonder. It was the third time this week they had dinner together. She finished washing their bowls and braced herself. If he'd lost a job, asking about the movies was already a disaster. "Hey Dad?"

Lawrence picked up a bowl and started drying it.

"How come you haven't started a new painting in so long?"

Lawrence looked up from the bowl and met her gaze. "What made you think of that?" He paused. "I guess it's because there's never enough time. I just got laid off at the factory yesterday, which is why I'm home early, and I guess now I'll have to start looking for another job." He set down both the bowl and the towel and paused. "The problem is two-fold. Not enough time, and not enough money. I am still trying to save some money to take you to the doctor, too."

"But Dad, you already have two other jobs." Brianna could hear herself whining.

"But, baby, those are just part time. They would never be enough to cover all of our expenses. Rent is expensive; groceries are expensive; life is expensive."

"So, I guess that means that I can't go to the movies on Friday?"

Lawrence noticed the tears welling up in Brianna's eyes. "Oh, baby, I'm so sorry, but movies are just an expense that I can't always provide for you."

"No, Dad, it's an expense that you can never provide for me." Brianna ran to her bedroom and slammed the door. As Lawrence stared after her, he could feel the shame burning his cheeks. He had suffered many indignities at a variety of humbling jobs, but they all paled to this. *Why can't I make ends meet enough to give my daughter twenty dollars on a Friday night?* He wanted her to have it; he knew it wasn't too much for her to ask to spend some time with her friends. What kid didn't want that? He wanted her to have everything; he worked so hard for *her*. Two or more jobs, every day, seven days a week. He almost never stopped working except to sleep, and he really didn't even get much of that.

Ever since Lawrence had decided to raise her on his own, he'd known it would be an uphill battle. He made that decision at sixteen and knew he wouldn't be able to finish high school. His only family were a dad who drank all the time and an older brother. He had no idea where his brother was now. He split a long time ago because he was tired of living with their drunken dad. Brianna's mother, Alexis, had been sixteen as well. She was addicted to heroin by the time Brianna was a year old, and Lawrence knew he couldn't leave the baby with her. He felt the only thing to do was to raise Brianna himself even though he didn't know the first thing about raising a baby. When he offered to take Brianna, Alexis couldn't get rid of her fast enough. Now, he felt distressed as he stared at her closed bedroom door. He had hoped that his sacrifices would give her the start to life that she deserved and he never had.

Brianna was three when Lawrence heard from an old acquaintance that Alexis died. Such a waste; she would have been only 19 years old. Brianna deserved a better mom. After her death, Lawrence would describe Alexis to Brianna as the mom she should have been. Her mother had wanted her, but she died, and Lawrence raised her by himself ever since. He hated lying to Brianna, and other than this one exception, he never did. He always wanted to be honest with her, but he didn't want her mother's weakness to define her. Other than that, he didn't keep anything from Brianna. They had been close since she was a baby. After all, it had always been just the two of them.

He stepped toward her bedroom door and leaned silently against it. Lately, he felt a distance growing between them and ever since he picked up that third job he could feel the gap widening. For now, it was nice to be laid off. He got to spend more time with Brianna and even have dinners together. But, it wouldn't be long until mounting bills would force him into another job, and they would go back to being passing ships in the night. He tried to enjoy the time he had with her now, but he felt a heaviness in his heart knowing that it wouldn't last for long. *And what good is it now anyway? She isn't even talking to me.*

Brianna surprised him by asking about his painting. He looked around at all of the artwork that adorned the walls of their tiny apartment. He used to finish a new painting almost every week. He painted everything, but mostly pictures of Brianna and the big house they would live in some day. Together, they made up stories about what their lives would be like and then he would paint it. A bittersweet smile curved his lips at the memory.

They survived on two jobs for a long time, but a third job became necessary a few years ago. As Brianna got older, it cost more to raise her. She needed more clothes, and she required more and more food. He never complained. There was nothing in the world that made him happier than taking care of his daughter. She was everything to him, but he never counted on just how hard it would be to raise all of the money and to raise her too. Now, it seemed he never had enough, and it outwardly disappointed Brianna. The emptiness of both the refrigerator and her closet reminded him of this daily.

He never really learned to live with the ever-present guilt that he felt. It was hard to know what bothered him more. The guilt that he never had enough money for her rivaled the guilt that he never had enough time. It ate him up on the inside, even when it wasn't his primary focus. But tonight, it wasn't for lack of focus. Tonight, the guilt sat front and center and would not let go of the stranglehold it had on him. Tonight, the guilt hit him over the head with an iron pipe. Tonight, they actually had some time to spend together, but she didn't want to be with him. Her anger and disappointment were too much. *Where did I go wrong? Why can't I give her everything she needs? What good is life if you don't have money?*

He got down on both knees and prayed.

***

Jack lay flat on his bed and stared at the ceiling. The crippling pain seared his thighs. He groaned. *This must be what sciatica feels like.* He'd heard enough people complain about it but never fully appreciated the agony. Worse, the muscle relaxants weren't as helpful as they were a few days ago.

He had taken a sleeping pill before bed, but apparently, that had worn off too. He turned his head to look at the clock. 3:33am. He thought about calling Amanda, but he was afraid he'd received her message all too clearly. She hadn't accepted his calls for a few days now. He supposed she'd issued an unspoken ultimatum. She probably wouldn't take his calls again unless he showed up with a ring.

At this particular moment, he couldn't even figure out how to stand up to go to the bathroom, much less get down on one knee with a ring. More than ever, Jack did not want Amanda to see how much he'd deteriorated. He would rather die than let her see how weak he had become. He used his arms to raise himself into a sitting position and pain rippled through his back. He cringed as he gently swung his legs off the side of the bed and onto the floor. He hobbled over to the bathroom to relieve himself and stumbled back into bed and back into the only position that was endurable.

He hadn't been in this much pain since he tore his ACL when he was a kid. Back in high school when he played lacrosse, he'd had a pretty serious collision with a player from another team that resulted in his leg folding up underneath him in impossible ways. When he had tried to stand up on the field, the pain shot through his leg and towards his back. It was the first time as a teenager he could not fight back tears. He found himself crying in the middle of the lacrosse field, in front of his teammates, the other team, and all of the spectators. Luckily, the paramedics came to rush him away from the humiliation. Doctors had eventually fixed his ACL, but he never fully recovered from what would follow at home.

He cringed now, not sure if it was from the back pain or the memory. Surgery on his knee left him in bed for the next two weeks. Isadora had worked hard to take care of him. She made all of his favorite foods and kept him stocked with new books and magazines to help pass the time. His sister Melissa told him about what he had missed at school and let him know that all of his friends wished him well and couldn't wait for him to come back. Even the boy from the other team, who he had collided with and had managed to escape with no injuries, sent him a get-well card.

But his mother wouldn't tolerate such coddling. No son of hers was going to be weak, and she needed him to prove to her that he wasn't. She had spent an extraordinary amount of money to ensure that he had the best surgeon in the world. Didn't he know that most kids in his position wouldn't have even been able to afford surgery, let alone the best?

"Why are you still in bed?" His mother stood in the doorway of his bedroom.

"Well, the doctor said…" Before he could finish his sentence, she interrupted him.

"You are never going to get strong unless you use your knee." She grabbed him by the shoulders and pulled him off his bed. His knee protested, pain flaring through the still-healing ligament. "Be strong," she demanded.

"Mother, please!" he yelled. He saw Isadora standing in the doorway, looking alarmed.

"Please, ma'am, let me help." Isadora ran to his aide.

"No, Isadora, you baby him too much. He is a man, not a little baby. He needs to get out of this bed and stop acting like one. If he's going to get strong, he'd better start using that knee."

Jack couldn't help himself; he started to cry again and collapsed back down on the bed, the pain engulfing him.

His mother's perfectly manicured hand smacked him across the face. "You need to stop acting like a baby right this minute. Get up! How in the world do you think you'll get strong by lying in bed?"

Jack tried with all his might to stand up, but he couldn't.

"You bring me nothing but shame." She stomped out of his bedroom.

Isadora rushed to his side and helped him back into bed. She put her hands over his knee, her lips moving almost without sound. From the few words Jack could make out, she was praying that his mother hadn't done too much damage to it. She'd been there. She had heard what the doctor said. He was very clear about Jack staying off of his knee for the first couple of weeks. His mother had no idea what she might have done, or further damage she might have caused. She hadn't bothered to be there to talk to the doctor.

Jack buried his face in his pillow, ashamed of the tears running down his face. "There's no reason to be ashamed, Jack. It takes courage to cry." Isadora brought him a glass of water. "Does it hurt very much?"

Jack just shook his head angrily. "Please just leave me alone."

Forty-five years later, the shame of that day felt as haunting and raw as it had then. As he lay in his bed, he tried with all his might to stand up. His back felt like it was on fire. He got to his feet. Pain swept through him until it turned to nausea. He couldn't make it to the bathroom before he was sick. Throwing up on his bedroom floor, he fell, almost face first, into his vomit. He was not a man; he was weak.

***

"What did you get for number eight?"

Brianna looked back at number eight on her homework and said "168."

"Crap!" Erin shouted. "I got 212. Why can't I figure this stuff out?"

Brianna took Erin's paper. "Let's see what you did wrong."

Erin's mother entered the room with a plate of cookies as Brianna was looking over her friend's paper. "You girls okay?"

"If you mean other than the fact that I'm colossally stupid, then yes, we're fine." Erin picked up a cookie and jammed it into her mouth.

"Erin, don't say that." Her mother stood over her and stroked her hair.

Brianna often wondered what life would be like if she had a mother in her life. Erin complained about her mom a lot, but Brianna knew how close they were. Brianna reached up and touched her own hair and thought about her own mother. She couldn't remember her at all. Her dad used to have an old snapshot of her years ago, but it had been a long time since she'd seen it. It might not even be around anymore.

Brianna returned to focus on Erin's paper. "Oh, look. Here's where you went wrong. Let me show you."

Erin's mother kissed the top of her head and left the room.

"Thanks, Brianna, but I'm sure I'm never going to get it." Erin hesitated then added, "You know, if you think you want to come to the movies with us this weekend, I can give you enough to go. I got a little extra allowance money this week."

Brianna leaned over her math book and intensely focused on her homework.

***

The sound of the phone woke him from his unconsciousness. As Jack opened his eyes, he groaned as he recalled why he was on the floor. He tried to push himself up, but the pain buckled his arms, and he fell back down into the dried puddle of vomit. He rolled onto his back in order to get a look at the clock on the nightstand. It was well after noon on Saturday. They had to have been wondering about him at the hospital. He scooted himself closer to the bed and was somehow able to pull himself up on his feet. He sat on the edge of the bed and looked at his phone. Amanda. He was relieved to see that it was her. He'd really missed her and thought maybe he had lost his chance with her forever. He figured he probably had a lot of explaining to do. He would eventually make it up to her, but not in his current state. He just had to get through this first. *She can't see how truly pathetic I am.*

He picked up the phone and called her back. She answered on the first ring. "Jack? Are you okay?"

"Yeah, sure, why?" He tried to mask his pain with his casual tone.

"A couple of people from the hospital called me this morning. They said they haven't been able to reach you. They've been calling you all morning. They mentioned some scheduled surgeries that you missed. I guess they thought I might know something, but obviously I don't."

Jack groaned inwardly. Why had they involved her? "Oh, yeah, I told them I wasn't going to be coming in this morning. I guess there must have been some sort of a mix-up."

Amanda was silent for a moment. "Is everything okay? It's not like you to miss work."

Jack cleared his throat and tried to find a comfortable spot on the bed. "Yeah, I just had some, uh, personal things to take care of." He cringed at how vague and unattached he sounded. He knew she wouldn't buy this bullshit.

"Personal?" Amanda waited for an explanation.

Jack was silent.

"Look, Jack, are you breaking up with me?" Amanda went straight to the point.

Jack felt tears spring to his eyes. He couldn't believe he was putting her through this. "No, honey, I don't want to lose you." His heart ached from his predicament. He didn't know if it was easier to lose her now or to wait for her to find out what a weakling he was and lose her then anyway.

"Let's have dinner tonight and we'll talk about it then." Amanda had had enough and wasn't going to waste any more time. It was now or never, and Jack wasn't going to get off so easily.

Jack stared at the mess of vomit on his bedroom floor. Until he figured out what was wrong with him, he would not see her. He had to be strong first. Her ultimatum couldn't have come at a worse time, but he really didn't have the energy to make a decision about it.

"Amanda, I really can't tonight." Jack could barely get the words out. He squeezed his eyes shut as he waited for her reaction.

"You're an asshole." Amanda hung up on him.

Jack lay back down on the bed. Maybe he needed to see a doctor, but first he needed to call into work and fix that mess.

***

Amanda sat and stared out of her window at the city below. She watched without really noticing the people and taxis rushing by. A single tear escaped her eye as she thought about how much she loved Jack. The heartache was unbearable, but she couldn't make him love her. She couldn't make him let her in. She fiercely loved him for many years and had always hoped she could somehow win him over and get under his thick skin, at least a little. But now, as she stared at the bustling world outside, she'd never felt so stuck. She and Jack had come too far to turn back, but on the other hand, they had run out of things to look forward to. The pain of her unrequited love, which knew no bounds, rivaled the pain of being alone and her desire to move on. She no longer had a choice. She had to free herself of this torture. Amanda pulled her knees defensively into her chest and took a sip of her tea. She knew what she had to do.

***

Jack managed to kiss enough ass over the phone to dig himself out of the pile of shit he created by not showing up for his surgeries. He really wasn't sure what would have happened if he hadn't been able to talk his way out of it, since he was physically incapable of moving. Mercifully, the muscle relaxant seemed to be controlling his pain, and he felt well enough to at least schedule a doctor visit next week. Maybe he should try to face Amanda now, clean up the mess he made with her. *I should just marry her. It's not like I can live without her.* He couldn't help but think she was crazy for wanting to be with him. Besides being a doctor, he had never really amounted to very much. He was a screw-up who blew every relationship he'd ever had with anyone.

He showered and made himself presentable before he picked up the phone and called. Eagerly, he waited for Amanda to answer, but instead all he got was unanswered ringing. He sighed. *Why wouldn't she avoid my calls at this point?* Maybe it was just as well. *Who am I kidding? I'm not going to be very good company anyway. Until a doctor can successfully tell me what's causing this pain and prescribe me the right treatment, I'm better off being alone.*

He wandered into his living room and looked at the shelves behind the bar that housed his expansive collection of expensive liquors. He settled on a bottle of scotch and pulled it down. As he moved, he felt something pull in his back. The pain shot up to his neck forcing him to drop the bottle. The amber liquid splashed over the onyx countertop and poured onto the floor. He stared as the twenty-year-old scotch seeped into the crevices of his drawers and cupboard doors…

He could hear his mother screaming in his ears. They were just sitting down for breakfast. The maids had served grapefruit juice but Melissa decided she wanted orange juice. She slid her chair away from the dining table and headed for the kitchen.

"Just where do you think you're going, young lady?" Mother hissed at Melissa.

"I'd just like to get myself some orange juice." Melissa looked down at her feet.

"First of all, you're being insolent. You didn't even excuse yourself from the table, and besides that, I'm sure Isadora or one of the others would be happy to help you with that." Mother picked up her napkin and placed it demurely in her lap.

Melissa met her mother's gaze. "Oh, but I really don't mind getting it myself, Mother. May I please be excused for a moment?"

Mother stared at Melissa for another second and nodded her head, ever so slightly. "Go on, but hurry up. It's rude to keep us waiting."

Melissa bounced out of the room and headed for the kitchen. Seconds later she reappeared holding a pitcher of orange juice. "Isadora was just finishing it up. Freshly squeezed." Melissa walked into the room, holding the pitcher up for everyone to see, when suddenly she tripped on the rug. She fell forward and the pitcher tumbled through the air. Jack glanced over at his horrified mother just as the pitcher smashed to the floor dousing his mother with orange juice and splashing onto her face.

Irate, Mother stood up from the table, gasping and wiping the burning, acidic juice from her eyes with her napkin. "What on earth have you done? Are you insane?"

Melissa's eyes filled with tears. "Mother, I'm sorry. It was an accident."

Mother's face turned bright red and quivered with anger. "This is exactly why I told you to wait for Isadora to bring it." She clenched her jaw together as she spat the words through her teeth. "You are a worthless child who can't even figure out how to carry a pitcher of orange juice." Mother stared at Melissa with wide, unforgiving eyes. "You will spend the rest of the morning cleaning this up." She

67

stomped from the room and turned back in the doorway.
"You are just as worthless as your father was."

Isadora appeared with a broom and began to sweep
up the glass fragments, but Mother forcefully intervened and
hysterically shooed her away. "No Isadora, you are not to
touch anything in here. Melissa is to clean the entire room.
She will pick up the glass and clean up this orange juice.
After that, she will put the breakfast away and clean every
last dish from this table. When she's done with that, she
will wash and iron the tablecloth. If I find out that anyone
helped her with any of it, so help me God..." Mrs. Parker
turned on her heel and headed up the stairs to her bedroom.

Jack shuddered now at the memory. He
wanted to protect Melissa when their mother was
being so cruel, but his mother terrified him to the
point of paralysis. Isadora would often try to
diffuse conflict, but her voice fell on deaf ears;
there was little she could do. When Mother made
up her mind about something, her word was final.
Any arguing with her just brought on more
punishment.

After Father died, her irrationality
worsened. Mother had been furious with him after
his death because it only reinforced how weak he
was. It was then she decided that her children
reflected his weakness too, and there was nothing
they could do to change that because their father's

blood ran through their veins. She reminded them on an almost daily basis of their affliction and made sure they remembered that life would always be hard for weaklings like them. No one would ever want them. Take it from her, marrying their father had been the worst decision she had ever made.

Jack mopped up the spilled scotch from the bar and floor. Even after the scotch had been cleaned up, he continued to scrub and scrub. He became so focused on cleaning that he no longer noticed his back pain. Once he was sure he cleaned it thoroughly, he went into the laundry room and found a gallon of bleach. He doused the bar with the bleach and cleaned it again, just to be sure.

Even though his mother had been gone for many years, he was sure she would have approved of his clean bar. He opened a new bottle of scotch and poured himself three fingers. Glass in hand, he found himself heading toward the drawing room and ultimately to the piano. He cringed as he sat down but before long he began to play. The songs came back with an ease that surprised him, as many years had passed since he'd played anything at all. He played for an hour or two. When he finally stood up to go to bed, he could have sworn that maybe his back felt a little better.

On his way upstairs, his doorbell rang and knew immediately it was Amanda. *Why didn't she just let herself in?* He took the stairs back down, two at a time, and threw the door open. His heart soared as he saw her beautiful presence standing on his front porch. His work was cut out; he had a lot to make up for these past few weeks but was eternally grateful to have her here in front of him. He threw his arms around her and pulled her tightly into an embrace.

"I'm so happy you're here."

To Amanda, he felt warm and safe, but she couldn't let herself fall back into his trap. Every breath she could feel on her neck seduced her yet also reminded her of the pain.

Her heart jumped to her throat, knowing what she had to do but didn't want to.

"Jack, I need to talk to you." This would be their last night together. It was excruciating being around him and to feel everything that came along with that, especially as they held each other. She no longer would fluctuate between loneliness and forced interaction, and she must explain that to him.

Jack pulled her in even more tightly. "Don't say anything."

As she continued to feel his arms around her, she knew it would be the last time. She blinked away tears as her heart filled with dread. She willed Jack not to let her go.

"Well then, change my mind." Her tears fell onto his shirt. *Doesn't he know that I will never come back?* She hadn't yet figured out how she would leave, because she truly didn't want to believe it would end. *Should I run out and never look back? Should I linger in the door for a moment and hope he'll beg me not to leave?* That possibility was the most frightening. If she did linger, she knew the begging would never come. *Will he silently watch me leave?* Paralyzed with indecision, she lingered in his arms a while longer, but her desperate white-knuckled cling to what they used to have was becoming embarrassing.

Jack held Amanda as if he would never let go. He loved her more than he ever had before and pulled her still more closely into himself. He could never be enough for her, petrified with the fear that he would let her down and not be able to protect her. He would make this sacrifice for her. He could never be what she wanted. He could never be what she needed. He could never be what she deserved.

He meekly whispered, "I can't."

He was tired of hiding his demons. He hadn't yet allowed Amanda into what he let happen to Melissa and the shame that destroyed him daily. He knew deep down he never would. He felt Amanda pull away and saw a tear fall down her cheek just before she quickly brushed it away. The look in her eyes was enough to kill him, and worse, she probably thought he was indifferent to it. Maybe it was better if she believed that. He averted his eyes, afraid they would give him away.

Brokenhearted, he allowed what he knew what would happen next and steeled himself to it.

Amanda moved to step back through door and turned her back to him. She stepped back onto the porch, and Jack felt his life flash before his eyes. He counted the years and the months and the days and the moments that he once had with her and couldn't believe it was ending this way. *Say something. Please, words. Say something. Say anything. Don't let her go. Don't let her go.* He had to let her go. He had to protect her.

Amanda took another step and another. Gracefully, she got into the cab that awaited in his driveway. Jack had never before felt as destroyed, as he watched the taillights disappear for what he knew would be the last time. At the time when it may have mattered most in his life, he decided to stand down. Impotent and broken. *Please God, just put me out of my pathetic misery.*

Chapter 4

As Nancy and Claire walked into Amy's home with their usual arsenal of groceries, the stale, yet unmistakable smell of cigarettes greeted them. *Oh no, what did she do now?* Bewildered, Nancy walked around the house, afraid of what she might find. "Amy?"

Horrified, Claire stayed by the door. Of course there was no answer from Amy. Nancy walked into the kitchen and spotted an ashtray full of cigarette butts. "Amy?" *What is going on here? Where is she?* Panic started to creep in. She walked further into the house toward Amy's bedroom. She gasped and dropped her bag of groceries.

"Amy!" She ran to her sister who laid awkwardly on the floor near the bed. "Please tell me you didn't hurt yourself." Nancy reached for Amy's wrist to check for a pulse and put her face near hers to feel any sign of breathing. Nancy shook her hard. "Amy!"

Amy snorted a little and fluttered her eyes open. "What happened?"

Nancy pulled her into a huge bear hug, stifling the urge to sob. "Oh thank God. I thought something had happened to you. I thought maybe you hurt yourself or something stupid like that."

Amy hiccupped and started to laugh.

"What the hell is so funny?"

"Oh, I remember now why I'm on the floor. I fell out of the bed, and I couldn't figure out how to get back up, so I just went back to sleep here." More belly laughs emerged from Amy.

"But it's seven o'clock in the evening. What…" Nancy looked around the room and spotted two empty vodka bottles. "My God, Amy, you're drunk. Did you drink all of this by yourself? You could've killed yourself with that much vodka!"

Claire, who watched from just outside the bedroom door, gasped in horror and stared at her daughter.

"Amy, do you have any idea what you're doing to me?" Claire turned on her heel and darted toward the front door. She let herself out and lingered on the porch. Nancy assumed her mother had gone out there to pout. God forbid their mother actually try to help when things got hard. Nancy reluctantly left Amy on the floor and followed her mother outside.

"What would your eighty-five-year-old grandmother think of this? This is just shameful behavior."

Nancy rolled her eyes at her mother's dramatics. "Mom, she's in serious pain. We can't just ignore what's going on."

Claire stamped her foot a little. "How do you think this makes me feel? Have you stopped to consider that she's only doing this to hurt me?"

Nancy stared at her mother as she tried to figure out what the hell she just said. "Mom, what are you talking about? Amy needs our support now, not our judgment. And I guarantee you this has nothing to do with hurting you."

Claire began to lose her temper, obviously uncomfortable by the direction the conversation was taking. "Look, Nancy, I know she lost something very valuable to her."

"She lost…" Nancy couldn't even bring herself to finish the sentence. "Mom, she didn't lose a pair of diamond earrings. What is wrong with you?"

Nancy left Claire on the porch and headed back to Amy's bedroom. She knew it would be weeks before her mother would forget her nonsupport. Claire probably wouldn't speak to her again until she apologized, and even then, their conversation would suffer for weeks. But right now, mom could wait. She had to deal with her sister. She picked up the bag of groceries and headed toward the kitchen. As Nancy entered the room, she looked around in disgust. *When had Amy picked up smoking?* This was obviously much worse than she thought. After putting the groceries away, she began to clean the kitchen. She picked up the ashtray from the kitchen table and dropped the entire thing in the garbage. She disappeared into the pantry and came out with a bag of coffee beans. Hot coffee would sober Amy up long enough to knock some sense into her. This had gone on long enough - too long apparently. As she watched the coffee brew, she tried to think how everything had become so awful.

When Nancy went back into the bedroom she found Amy passed out again but this time in the bed. She shook her awake. "Sit up!"

Amy glared at her and rolled over.

Nancy shook her violently. "I'm serious Amy, SIT UP."

Amy resumed her glare. "What is your problem?"

"What is *my* problem? What is *your* problem?" Nancy stared at her, furious. "You're killing yourself!"

"What is *my* problem? What is *my* problem? What do you think? My son's dead!" Amy screamed at her sister. "I left my whole world behind when I left him at that cemetery. I completely failed as a mother. If there is one thing that a mother should be responsible for, it's that your child should not die. They should lock me up and throw away the key! I hope I do die!"

Nancy paused for a moment and remembered the coffee mug in her hand.

"Here," Nancy pressed the cup of strong black coffee into Amy's hands. "Drink."

Nancy crawled into the other side of the bed and lay quietly beside her sister for a few minutes. "Amy, this is not good. And by the way, no one needs to lock you up. You seem to have done a pretty good job of that yourself."

"What?"

"You can't just hide from life forever, and you certainly can't do it by day drinking and smoking cigarettes, or you really will end up killing yourself."

"Hide from what life? Jonathan was my life. He's gone, so there's nothing left for me. People sometimes die of broken hearts. I've heard of that before. Why can't that kind of mercy be given to me? I just want to lie down next to my son." Amy's tears fell into the hot coffee.

Her statement jolted Nancy. Shame swept over her as she listened to her sister. She knew she grieved the loss of her son, but this was the first time hearing that Amy felt she had nothing left to live for. Nancy knew she pushed Amy away enough times in their lives to not be important to her, but it still hurt to realize that she wasn't enough to keep her sister from wanting to die.

"Nothing left? What about Luke?"

At the mention of Luke's name, Amy's hands shook so hard the coffee began to spill. "Do not speak his name to me! Do you have any idea what he's done?"

Nancy took the coffee from Amy's hand before she could spill any more and placed it on the bedside table. "No, Amy. I have no idea what he's done because you haven't talked to me, or anyone else, since Jonathan died. Maybe you could at least try to explain to me what's going on. Maybe there's even a small chance I could help."

Amy looked at Nancy and started to laugh.

Oh great, Nancy thought, *she's still drunk.* "Maybe I'll come back later to talk."

Amy put her hand on Nancy's shoulder. "I just always thought that no matter what happened to Jonathan, I could fix it." Nancy was surprised that Amy was talking at all, let alone coherently. Amy laid her hands in her lap and Nancy watched them tremble. "Even when he got sick, I just thought if I worked hard enough and did everything the doctors said, that I could make him better. It was my job to protect him. I brought him into this world, and he trusted me to protect him. That's what children do; they trust their mothers to protect them. I let him down in the most paramount way. I let him down in the worst way. I will never forgive myself for that; I keep looking for a small opening, anything, to try to escape this labyrinth of hell I'm in, but I can't find any way out. And Luke is largely to blame for this. How could I possibly forgive him?"

Nancy grabbed Amy's shaking hands and squeezed them.

Amy went on. "I never told you about the last conversation that Luke and I had before Jonathan died. It was actually an argument."

Nancy held her breath. She had been waiting for her sister to talk to her about this, but now that the moment was here, she wasn't sure she was ready. The idea of Amy thinking that Luke had somehow caused Jonathan's death mystified her. He wouldn't do anything to hurt his son; he loved his son every bit as much as Amy had.

She was equally surprised to hear they argued. Amy and Luke almost never did. The two of them still appeared so in love after all of those years of marriage, it often left other married couples stupefied. They were the best of friends.

"He thought I coddled Jonathan because of his epilepsy. He thought we should start giving him a little more independence now that he was getting older. He accused me of hovering too much. He told me that nothing bad would come out of leaving him to be on his own for a while. I couldn't believe what he was saying. I was so angry that he was twisting everything around. He made it seem like being protective was somehow doing him harm or doing him a disservice. And on top of that, I couldn't believe that he didn't feel that protecting our son was important. It was like I was talking to a stranger. I told Luke that he was the one who was wrong, and that he needed to pay more attention, or one of these days Jonathan was going to have a seizure and get hurt." Amy's voice suddenly dropped lower. "It was only two days later that Luke left Jonathan alone and he decided to go swimming. I'm pretty sure you know how that story ends."

Nancy found herself holding her breath throughout the story, grateful to be talking to her sister for the first time in weeks.

"I was so angry with him that day. He didn't understand the gravity of what he was saying. He left Jonathan alone just to spite me and prove that he was right. Well, he wasn't right about anything. It's unforgiveable!" Amy wiped her nose on the sleeve of her bathrobe and repeated, "How could I ever forgive him?" She slumped over, pushed her face into her pillow, and sobbed.

Nancy stared at her sister, understanding now how crushing the enormity of the weight of all that she carried was. She struggled for words.

"Amy, I know Luke enough to know…"

Amy snapped her head up to look at Nancy. "What do you know? Were you about to defend him? You don't know anything about us." Amy seethed. "How dare you pretend to know anything? I barely know you; we never talk. You're so busy with your god-damned career. We were lucky to see you at Jonathan's birthday parties. You hardly knew any of us, and yet you're going to pretend to be a sister. Well, you can't have it both ways. You can't ignore me your whole life and then come in here thinking you have all the answers when my child dies. You don't have the slightest clue of what I'm going through or what I need. Every night I pray that I will not live to see the sun rise. Some days I just want to burn the house down while I'm still in it. I don't even know why you're here." Amy sat up and turned away. "I think you need to leave me alone."

Reeling from Amy's verbal punch, Nancy tried to recover and catch her breath. She breathed in and out a few times, cleared her throat, and stood up and left. She knew the depths of her sister's suffering caused her to say those things, but deep down, they both knew she was right.

Nancy backed out of the room and heard her mother in the kitchen. She found Claire bent over the sink, scrubbing. Nancy joined her and started to give her a hand. Claire just waived her off.

"I'll do it, Nancy. I do everything around here anyway." She sighed loudly as she continued cleaning.

Nancy couldn't believe her ears. Infuriated, she stormed out of the house.

***

Jack laid in bed. By now he had memorized every mark on the ceiling. His bladder ached and called for him to get up, but the pain in his leg and back were so excruciating he wasn't sure if he could do it. *Didn't I just go to the bathroom?* He'd been sleeping on and off all day and this was the fourth time this evening he'd had to get up and pee. He moved to the edge of the bed and gingerly placed his feet on the floor. Limping slowly to the bathroom, he managed to relieve himself once again.

His mind wandered to a conversation he'd had with his friend Justin that morning. He and Justin had been friends since they were residents, and now, later in their careers, they worked together in the university hospital for the last ten years. He was a heart surgeon like Jack, but he had agreed to take a look at Jack's back problem. Not wanting to draw any attention to himself at the hospital, Jack knew he could trust Justin to be discreet. When Justin thought it could be a problem with the vertebrae or pelvis, he suggested an x-ray. The idea caught Jack off guard. All this time, he figured a nerve had been causing his pain. He never considered that it might be bone related. As he stood before the toilet, he contemplated what that might mean, but he didn't really want to think about it. He limped back to the bed and slowly lay back down. He felt his eyelids closing…

He held a martini in the middle of a social gathering, surrounded by unfamiliar faces, most of them self-righteous. He introduced himself to the man standing next to him. They shook hands and exchanged niceties. The man began to complain that his neighbor's house recently sold for only $2.4 million. "There goes the neighborhood," he grumbled into his drink. "I guess they'll let just anyone in these days." Jack glanced around the room to avoid the awkward silence that was settling in, and he spotted a person who looked exactly like himself across the room. The man he'd just introduced himself to followed his gaze.

"Is that your twin?"

Jack sipped his martini and turned to look at his new acquaintance. "That's John. He never made anything of himself. I'm a highly successful surgeon, and my brother over there never became anything other than a drunk."

Jack turned his gaze back to John and as he did he noticed something in his hands. As he looked more closely, he realized that his twin brother casually whittled wood. Out of nowhere, John turned the knife on himself, and before Jack could even react, blood began to drip from his brother's wrists.

Jack awoke and tried to shake off the dream. He couldn't make much sense of it. He never had a brother at all, much less a twin. Shuddering at the still haunting visual, he couldn't stop the memories of his sister from flooding in. He used every bit of strength to tamp them down, but it was too late. Thoughts of Melissa controlled his mind.

He could feel the pressure in his bladder again. Jack forced himself out of bed for the fifth time that night, hoping it would alleviate the thoughts of Melissa. He shuffled to the bathroom and angrily shoved the memories away, but they broke the dam he built to keep them at bay.

He was eighteen and had just that week been accepted to Yale. His mother, in a rare moment of elation, agreed to let him go out with friends to celebrate his acceptance. He'd just come back from a quiet reflective visit to his favorite place, the old secluded bridge, to think about what lay ahead for him and his future. He called his friend Mike and told him he would pick him up just as soon as he took a shower.

The door to the bathroom that he shared with his sister had been locked, and he waited for over an hour. Growing impatient he began banging on the door. Another forty-five minutes went by with no answer, and Jack finally decided to break in the door.

Her body was motionless, but he didn't realize what he had encountered. "Melissa?" He saw her limp body floating in a sea of red. Shock and dread mingled in his head. Slow realization began to take over as he understood all too well what had happened. "Melissa!"

With trembling hands, he grabbed his sister and tried to pull her out of the tub. "Mother! Isadora! Help!"

He grabbed her under her shoulders and tried to lift her from the tub, but she kept slipping out of his hands. Isadora made it up the stairs to find Jack hysterical and pulling a bloodied Melissa from the bath water. Isadora ran from the room to call an ambulance…but it was too late. Melissa was gone. The image burned into him, promising to be with him forever. It was a bell he would never un-ring.

Jack got back into bed and stared at the same spot on the ceiling again. The images of the nightmare pulsed through his mind, the bleeding man emblazoned in his brain. As he lay there, trying to push the images away, he remembered a recurring dream he would have as a child, maybe around seven years old. The dream was always the same. He had a twin in the dream, an identical little boy. They were at an amusement park and they would excitedly jump into the cars of a roller coaster together. But, when the ride would start and Jack's car began to move forward, his twin's car would start pulling away from him and begin to travel backward.

Jack shuddered again and leaned over to the night table for his sleeping pills. He really couldn't bear to be alone, and he reached for his phone to call Amanda.

Amanda checked her phone's display as she flopped down on her couch. *Why is he calling me?* She let it go to voicemail. With other things on her mind now, she didn't want Jack to weasel his way into the equation. Tonight had been her fourth date with Derek, and she knew he must have been expecting something more than a kiss on the cheek when he dropped her off at her apartment, but she just didn't feel like inviting him in.

She restrained herself from calling Jack back. As much as she wanted to talk to him, she wasn't going to put herself through that anymore. Adrienne had been right; she had too much respect for herself to keep putting up with his games and lack of commitment. Sticking to her guns, she distracted herself with wine and television, but there was no distraction strong enough to keep her from her own demise.

"Oh, damn it."

She picked up her phone and called him back.

"Baby, I miss you." Jack sounded like he might have been crying.

"Jack, please. I can't do this anymore."

Jack was silent.

Amanda hesitated before she decided to tell him the truth. "I've been out with someone else."

"Is that what this is about?"

"Excuse me?"

"That's why you're breaking up with me? Because of some other guy?" Jack spat the words out. "Now it all makes perfect sense."

Amanda could feel the anger rising to her throat. "No, Jack, this is not about some other guy. This is about you not feeling the same way for me as I feel about you. This is about you not making a commitment to me, and worse, not even *wanting* to make a commitment to me. Did you think that I just wouldn't notice that you never were going to let me in? How long did you think that would last, Jack?"

"I will not be given an ultimatum. So, I guess we're finished here."

"You called me. Let's not forget that. But if it makes this easier for you to blame me, be my guest." Amanda took that moment to hang up the phone and sob into her glass of wine.

Jack stared blankly at his phone as he realized that Amanda just hung up on him. He breathed in and out, slowly, to calm his blood pressure. As angry as he was, he knew she was right. Something finally got through. Maybe it was the threat of another man, but he was suddenly jostled into the reality of just what he had done when it came to Amanda. This time, he knew what he had to do.

***

Brianna finished painting Julia's toenails and took a sip of her root beer. She had been so relieved when Erin had invited all the girls over for a sleepover at her house rather than going out to do something that required money. Last weekend, Erin saved the day again when they all decided to go out. She paid for her movie and didn't make a big deal out of it. And Brianna was *particularly* grateful to Erin that she didn't miss out on that *particular* trip to the movies because Mark had held her hand the whole time.

She focused her attention back to the movie they were watching in Erin's bedroom. The horror scene was just picking up speed. The young girl was running down the street looking over her shoulder, as the killer with the axe was limping along behind her. He began to catch up and was wielding the axe over his head, when Erin's cell phone blared a ringtone. All the girls screamed and collapsed into a pool of giggles when they realized what happened.

Erin grabbed the phone off the bed. "Hello?"

Erin shushed the girls' laughter. "Hi, Mark. What's up?"

Brianna felt the blood rush to her cheeks. *Why was he calling?*

"Sure, you guys can come over. We'll sneak you in through the basement." Erin hung up the phone. "Mark and the guys are hanging out, and they're on their way over here."

The girls squealed and hurriedly began changing from their pajamas back into their clothes. "I'll go make sure my parents are in bed and run a diversion if I have to. Run down to the basement and watch for the guys."

In a fit of giggles, they made their way downstairs and into the basement. Brianna's heart was pounding as she waited for the guys to show up. She wondered if she'd get a chance to be alone with Mark. She hadn't seen him much since he held her hand at the movies last weekend. The only class they had together was gym, but since she was excused from that until a doctor evaluated her, they hadn't had a lot of opportunity to see each other outside of lunch. Butterflies fluttered in her stomach, and her anxiety grew worse by the minute. *Could he possibly still be interested in me?*

The other girls began shrieking; the boys must have arrived.

"Shhhh," Brianna said. "If Erin's parents hear you guys, we're all dead meat."

Julia flung the basement door open and the boys shuffled quietly in. Mark spotted Brianna and smiled at her. She beamed back at him.

Rob scoped out the basement and spotted the pool table. "Can we play?"

Erin came down the basement stairs. "Guys, my parents haven't gone to sleep yet, so we should probably be quiet."

Brianna piped up. "How about Truth or Dare?

Rob had a better idea. "How about spin the bottle?"

Brianna was still holding her root beer bottle. "I've got a bottle right here." She glanced over at Mark, and she thought he looked irritated.

Mark shifted his weight from foot to foot. "We could go outside and play flashlight tag."

"Yeah, let's do that." The boys loved that idea.

Erin shrugged. "Fine by me. Let me go get some flashlights."

Brianna followed the boys outside. Mark took her by the hand and led her off into the dark, away from the other kids.

Her heart was racing. "You didn't want to play spin the bottle?"

Mark squeezed her hand a little. "I didn't want to take the chance of one of my friends getting to kiss you before I did." Before she could respond, Mark's mouth was on hers and his tongue was pushing into her mouth. Brianna felt dizzy and didn't know what to do. The awkward kiss was wet and a little gross, but she couldn't help feeling happy about the whole thing.

"Are you okay?" Mark stopped and looked at her.

"Yeah, what do you mean?"

"I don't know, I was just checking. Because you fainted at gym, I thought maybe you were sick or something."

"Oh that. It's nothing. I'm fine." Brianna could feel her cheeks burning.

"There you two are." Erin was right next to them shining a flashlight in their faces. "Oh my God, am I interrupting something?"

Mark punched Erin on the shoulder. "No, you're not interrupting anything. You better start running because I'm it." The girls took off screaming. Brianna grabbed Erin by the hand as they ran together into the dark neighborhood. Mark was getting closer and closer. That was the last thing Brianna remembered before falling face first into the street.

Chapter 5

Jack stared blankly at Justin, who held the results of his x-ray.

"A lesion on the proximal femur?" Jack sat up straighter in Justin's office. That was the last thing he expected to hear.

Justin was pensive for a moment, and his eyes gave away what he would to say next. "I'm ordering an MRI to assess the extent."

"Oh, come on Justin! Don't treat me like a patient. Just tell me what you saw." Jack was feeling more nervous now.

"It seems that part of it is more aggressive than the rest. The aggressive part shows a destructive pattern of growth and it's adjacent to what looks like a cartilaginous tumor."

Jack inhaled sharply. "De-differentiated?"

"We don't know yet. Jack, don't get upset. Let's get the MRI and then I want you to talk to Harold in Oncology."

Jack jumped up from his chair. "I want to see the x-ray."

Justin put his hands up. "Okay, okay. Just stay calm." Justin reluctantly flipped on the switch of his lightbox and inserted Jack's x-rays.

As Jack stared at the images, his life flashed before his eyes. Justin had been generous in his description. He knew right away what he was looking it. The clear line of demarcation of the tumors was a sure-fire indicator that this was de-differentiated.

Justin put his hand on Jack's shoulder. "Talk to Harold. Get an open incisional biopsy. Let's find out the different histologic grades."

Jack pulled away from Justin, angry now. "Stop talking to me like that! I know what this is, and so do you."

"Jack, there are surgeries that can be done."

"Surgeries? They'd have to amputate my leg, Justin."

"Maybe not. There's always EPR." Jack knew Justin was grasping at straws.

"And besides, even if they cut off my leg, we both know that widespread metastasis is a sure thing here."

Justin put his hand on Jack's shoulder for the second time. "Okay, now you really are getting ahead of yourself. Just slow down. I can't say that yet. We need a full body scan." Justin was giving him the standard line. He hesitated and studied Jack's face carefully.

Of all the possibilities Jack had thought of to explain his pain, he'd never even considered this one. He couldn't feel anything; maybe he'd already gone into shock. He hoped so. When the room began to spin, Jack stood up and thought for a moment he might throw up. He knew as well as Justin that this was likely fatal.

"Jack, don't give up. We'll start chemotherapy right away. You know as well as I do the number of clinical trials the hospital is involved in. There are a number of things we can do."

Jack slowly and deliberately walked out of the office.

"Jack, don't give up." His friend yelled desperately after him.

Jack could barely hear what his friend had said; the loud whooshing in his ears was deafening.

He already knew what the body scan would say. He'd practiced medicine long enough to know how this was going to end. As he put one foot in front of the other, he walked blindly out of the hospital and toward his car. He already knew he might be looking at about a year left on his life, and that was only if he was lucky. He made it all the way to the parking structure before throwing up on the ground, while he stood holding onto the side of his Ferrari. He closed his eyes and tried to take some deep breaths in an effort to stop the panic from setting in. Fumbling to open his car door, he lowered his shaky body slowly onto the seat. He laid his head on the steering wheel and sobbed. More validation of just how weak he was.

He reached into his pocket for his cell phone. He needed Amanda now more than ever. She answered on the first ring.

"Hello, Jack. I'm asking you to please not call me anymore. It's too confusing. Every time I start to get over you, you call again, and that is just too painful. It's over, Jack. I need you to respect that. I need to be part of your past. I'm sorry." When Amanda hung up the phone, he wasn't sure he'd heard her right. The world seemed to be going on around him in slow motion as he watched his life circling the drain.

He couldn't remember driving home, but he realized he must have when he pulled his car into the garage. He drifted through his house in a surreal dream-like state and got into bed with his clothes still on. The pain in his back seemed to have somehow changed. He couldn't feel anything, actually; he was so stunned by the news that his mind seemed to have completely cleaved from his body.

Dazed, he laid on his bed for hours. He tried to retrace his steps to figure out how his life had turned out this way. He'd always envisioned himself as something else. He used to think he had it all, but the truth was he had nothing at all. He'd been too busy hiding from anything that ever really mattered. He stared at the familiar spot on the ceiling and brought his attention to his breathing. Inhale. Exhale. Inhale. Exhale. Inhale. Exhale. Concentrating just on his lungs, he wondered why he never had before. He gained a new appreciation for his likely cancer-riddled lungs and the fact that they were able to sustain his oxygen needs for all these years without ever even being conscious of it. Inhale. Exhale.

"Mother?" He could have sworn he had heard her yelling at him. He could still hear her in his ears. *"Stop being such a wimp and get up. You're embarrassing me."* He must have been dreaming of her. *Maybe I should get up. Maybe mother was right. I am a wimp.* Why couldn't he get out of bed? Inhale. Exhale. Inhale. Exhale.

The wave of childhood memories came as gently as a derailing train.

He was standing by the tennis court in their backyard, when his sister pulled up in the Porsche. His jaw dropped as she nonchalantly pulled the car into its spot in the garage.

"What were you thinking? Mother would kill you if…" Jack was unable to finish his sentence before he saw his Mother running down the driveway toward their ten-car garage.

"Young lady, get out of that car, right this minute!"
Mother was irate.

Apparently, Melissa was taking too long to get out of the car because the next thing Jack saw was Mother pulling Melissa out of the car by her hair and dragging her to the house. Melissa screamed in pain and terror. Mother pulled Melissa into the house and threw her to the kitchen floor.

Jack pressed the heels of his hands hard against his eyes to stop the movie screen of memories. His heart pounded agonizingly in his chest. Inhale. Exhale. Inhale. Exhale. He choked back a sob. *Stop being a baby. Stop crying. What is wrong with me? She was just trying to make us stronger, and we obviously needed it. I ended up a crybaby riddled with cancer, and Melissa ended up killing herself. Mother must have been right. We were both weak, just like our father. Mother was right all along.*

Inhale. Exhale. There was nothing left to do now but wait for death; he hoped it would come quickly.

***

Inhale. Exhale. Amy laid on her bed and stared at the ceiling, trapped forevermore in the hell of carrying the guilt and burden from not being able to protect her son. She thought about him drowning all alone, and how terrified he must have felt at the end. Tears filled her eyes as she thought of her son's last tortuous moments. There was nothing left to do now but die; she hoped somehow death would find her. Inhale. Exhale. Her chest rose and fell, but she failed to feel anything other than self-hatred. It was as if all the life had already been sucked out of her. Why she was still breathing was a cruelty to her. A cruel twisted punchline, because every other part of her died when Jonathan had. Her breath had become a curse.

There was a loud banging on the front door followed by several rings of the doorbell. Amy rolled over and pulled the pillow over her head. More banging, followed by more bells. *Go away. Why won't she just leave me alone?* Amy heard the sound of the key turning in the lock. *Why did I give Nancy that key? I need to get that back from her. She can't just keep coming in here like this.*

"Amy!"

Oh shit, that's not Nancy. That was definitely not Nancy. *What in the world is he doing here?* Amy sat up in bed and pulled out her armor, preparing for battle.

"Amy!"

Amy could hear him frantically running all around the house, looking for her. He finally made his way into the bedroom and saw her in the bed. Luke stood in the doorway, in his usual dress shirt and pants. He must either have been coming from or going to work. She wasn't sure since she had absolutely no idea what time of day it was. Luke worked as a financial analyst for years, and unless he was meeting with a client, he always wore essentially the same thing. The sight of him immediately induced a sour taste on her tongue. For a moment, she thought she might throw up, vile churning in her stomach. "Amy, what are you doing? Why are you in bed? Are you okay?"

Amy curled her hands into fists and bit her tongue. *How am I supposed to answer that?*

"Amy, you have to talk to me. Why aren't you taking any of my calls? I haven't talked to you in a month." Luke stood next to her by the bed.

"Get out! I told you that you are not welcome here! Why are you here?" Amy tried not to scream, but she couldn't help herself. Anger flooded over her.

"This is still my house, Amy." Luke was near tears.

"It's not. I kicked you out." Amy pouted like a child.

"I still pay the mortgage on this house, so I feel entitled to come in. I'm still married to you, so I feel entitled to find out how you are." She could hear the desperation in his voice, but she didn't care.

"Well, now you've done both, so I guess you can go now." Amy lay back down on the bed and pulled the covers over her head. "You should be grateful that you don't have to live here. You don't have to stare at his empty bedroom every day and have to see his empty chair at the kitchen table."

"Please talk to me. I'm dying without you." Luke sat on the bed next to her.

"Well, I'm dying without him, so I guess that makes us about even." Amy kicked him as hard as she could, and he fell off the bed.

Luke sat on the floor, stunned by her kick. He waited a few moments and eventually said, "I am living in the same hell that you are. I walk through the same fire that you do. I fucked up, Amy. I did. But how could I have ever known it would be at this price?"

He wanted to force Amy to talk to him, but he loved and respected his wife enough to give her the space that he knew she still needed. He didn't want to risk losing her even more by pushing her before she was ready. He stood up silently and brushed himself off as he left the room. He let himself calmly out of the front door and got back into his car, with no choice but to head back to the hotel he'd been staying in for weeks. Of course, he had friends offer him a place to stay, but somehow that seemed even more depressing than staying in the damned hotel.

How did we get here?

Amy blamed him for Jonathan's death, and some days, he convinced himself that she was right. Deep down, he really wasn't sure. Amy might have been right; he shouldn't have left Jonathan alone that day. He never would have thought in a million years that Jonathan would try to swim by himself; he only wanted to give his son a little space.

The truth was Amy had hovered over Jonathan from the minute he was born. After Jonathan came into their lives, Amy gave up all of her usual hobbies and interests and threw herself entirely into Jonathan's life. When he got a bad grade on a paper, she would call and argue with the teacher; when he lost a baseball game, she would get upset with the coach.

Luke always thought she was overprotective. He knew it was essential to let Jonathan learn by his own mistakes, but Amy was almost hysterical about keeping Jonathan protected from things until he was a little older.

After Jonathan was diagnosed with epilepsy, Amy became more hysterical than ever. She never let him out of her sight. He was no longer even allowed to hang out with his friends unless she was there. She dragged the poor kid from doctor's appointment to doctor's appointment, and was a worse helicopter mom than ever before.

Luke could feel Jonathan's tensions increasing and wanted to give his teenager a little more freedom. That fateful day when Amy had a dentist appointment, Luke used that to his advantage and let Jonathan know that he would be going out for about an hour, and that he would be in charge of the house for a while. The look on Jonathan's face had told Luke at the time that he'd made the right decision. Jonathan was elated. Luke realized that it may have been the first time in his fifteen years that Jonathan had been left alone.

Luke was feeling really happy for his son as he drove to the grocery store, thinking about the small amount of independence that his son had been so longing for. He knew he would have hell to pay with Amy when she got home, and he would have to tell her what he did, but he was prepared to defend his position. What he never anticipated was that Jonathan would go swimming at the neighbors' house.

Now as he started his car, he stared at his house. He remembered when they bought it. They were so young, and Jonathan wasn't even walking yet. Now, as he sat gazing upon the house, he realized there wasn't much left of it. It had been bulldozed by tragedy. He put his head in his hands and sobbed. *How did this happen? How could this have happened?*

He thought back to his college days when he first met Amy, when the two of them were put together for a physics project. He had loved her from probably the first time he saw her…

The group decided to meet at a coffee shop. His best friend and fraternity brother, Christopher, happened to be selected as part of the same group, so the two of them walked together and grabbed a table. He was hungover and not prepared for their group assignment, but he definitely wasn't prepared for Amy. A very attractive redhead with green eyes threw herself into the chair across from him.

"Physics 305?"

Luke and Christopher both nodded a yes. Christopher's bored. Luke's mesmerized.

"Sorry I'm late," she said.

Christopher looked at his watch. "You're not late. You're five minutes early."

"Oh, good, I'm going to get coffee then." She disappeared as quickly as she had appeared.

"Who was that?" Luke was stunned. How had he never noticed her before? Sure, it was a big lecture hall, but still, it seemed like he wouldn't have missed her.

Christopher glanced down at the list of names for their group. "According to this, she's either Jill or Amy."

They watched as another girl, this one familiar looking to them, joined the redhead in line. After a few minutes, they sat down together at the table.

"I'm Jill." The familiar looking girl introduced herself.

They exchanged introductions, and Amy sipped her coffee. They spent the next ninety minutes together talking about quantum mechanics. Luke found the topic to be excruciating and wondered why a finance major, such as himself, had to take physics, but having Amy there was making it much more pleasurable.

Luke spent the majority of that time trying to stare at Amy without her noticing. She was fascinating, even the way she drank her coffee captivated him. He couldn't turn his gaze as she brought the cup to her lips.

Later, as he and Christopher walked home together from the meeting, Luke couldn't get his mind off of Amy. He thought maybe he caught her looking at him, but he couldn't be sure, and he shouldn't be thinking that way anyway. The phone was ringing in their house as they let themselves in.

"Luke, you here? It's for you." One of his fraternity brothers was shouting from the living room. Luke jogged over to take the phone from him.

"Hey babe, it's me." It was his girlfriend of two years, Dawn.

Guilt washed over him. He should probably start thinking a little more about his girlfriend and less about Amy. "Hey, want to come over?"

"Can't - the house is having a meeting tonight."

"Tell the lovely girls of Kappa I said hi."

"Well, wait, what about tomorrow?"

"Can't - I have a meeting with my physics group tomorrow. It's a huge project, and we realized today how much time it's going to take to do it." He tried to sound annoyed, but actually, Luke didn't mind having to spend more time with Amy.

"How about after? Where will you be?"

"We're meeting at the library until probably 9:00 or so."

"That's fine. I'll meet you there."

Luke took longer than usual getting ready for the study group the next day. He changed his shirt three or four times and still felt like he wasn't happy with how he looked as he left for the meeting. He could feel his heart racing a little as he opened the door of the library. He looked around and saw that everyone, including Amy, was already there. He hurried over to the table.

Christopher took charge of the meeting. "Okay, so we have to describe why Einstein's work didn't disprove Newton, just that he discovered more truths, right? That shouldn't be that hard. I think we can handle this." He looked around the table, clearly hoping he sounded more confident than he felt.

Amy was inching out of her coat, and her arm brushed against Luke's. They briefly made eye contact, and he felt his stomach drop to his shoes. He could barely breathe. She glanced at him apologetically.

For the first hour, Luke couldn't concentrate because he was so distracted by Amy. Every time she brushed her hair off of her face, or picked up a pencil, or breathed. He kept saying Dawn's name in his head over and over as a distraction, but it wasn't very effective.

"So, if in quantum physics, space and time are meaningless, does it mean that the length of a minute could be different things to different people?" Jill was trying to wrap her head around the concept.

"Oh, definitely," Luke finally had something to contribute. "Let me give you an example. Let's say you're in a car with four people. Two of them have to go to the bathroom really bad, but you're still four miles from the next rest stop. The length of a minute will seem much longer to the two who need to pee."

Amy burst out laughing. Everyone else rolled their eyes at his joke.

"Or, if you've just put everything on red and you're waiting for that little ball to stop," Amy retorted.

"Or, if you've just been shot and you're waiting for an ambulance." Christopher and Jill just stared at them and moved on to the next topic. Amy and Luke exchanged a private glance and smiled at each other.

"I need a coffee break." Luke stood up and stretched. "I'll run out and get some. Who wants coffee?"

"I do bro, for sure." Christopher nodded enthusiastically as Jill waved off the offer.

"I'll go with you." Amy got up and stood next to Luke. "I kind of feel like stretching my legs."

As they walked the short distance to the coffee shop together, Amy didn't say much. Luke couldn't come up with anything witty to say, so he didn't talk much either. After they got the coffee and carried it back together, their conversation was infrequent again.

At five minutes to nine, Christopher slammed his book shut. "I think we've had enough." He leaned over to Luke. "Hey, buddy, do you want to grab a beer or something?"

"Not tonight, Chris; he's all mine." They all turned to see a stunning blonde standing next to them. She draped her arm around Luke's neck.

Luke glanced at Dawn and back to the group. "Everybody, this is Dawn." Luke glanced at Amy; he was pretty sure he saw her raise an eyebrow.

"Nice to meet you," Dawn said to no one in particular. She looked at Luke. "Ready?"

***

The next day, their physics group had been back at it again for a few hours. "Okay, the next part is The Schrodinger Equation and its components." Christopher groaned as he read it. "It already sounds too complicated."

Amy grabbed the paper from him. "I'm sure we can figure it out. Let's do what it says. First, we'll break it down into its components; maybe it will be easier to digest the whole thing then."

"I'm not digesting anything right now except maybe a sandwich." Christopher pushed his chair back from the table. "Anybody want to grab lunch?"

Jill pushed her chair back too. "Yeah, I actually have some stuff I need to do. Can we meet back here in a couple hours?"

It didn't take much to convince the group that they needed a break.

Luke noticed that Amy didn't say anything as she got up and walked away. He lingered behind for a moment wondering if that had anything to do with Dawn. As he left the library, he spotted Amy sitting under a tree and walked over to her. He shoved his hands in his pockets. "You alright?"

Amy shrugged. "I'm okay."

"You want some company?" Luke kicked at the ground a little with the toe of his shoe.

Amy looked up at him, surprised. "Sure."

Luke plopped down next to her and they were quiet for a while.

"Sometimes it helps to talk about it, if you want to."

Amy glanced over at him, feeling a little embarrassed about it now. "It's just a grade that's all."

Luke said nothing and listened.

"I got a D on an English paper, which is really unusual for me. I mean, I probably deserved it because I didn't work very hard on it, but it's still a little shocking."

"Don't be so hard on yourself. Nobody's perfect." Luke tried to make her feel better.

"Oh, it's not really that. It's my mom, mostly. She's always hanging over my head the fact that she's paying for my college education. She's threatened many times that if my grades fell at all, she would cut me off."

"Whoa, that's pretty rough." Luke was quiet for a moment. "Do you think she'd really do that?"

"I'm not sure, but I don't really want to find out. On the one hand, my mom is really concerned about how things look to the outside world, so a bad grade would definitely be a disgrace in her book, but on the other hand, if I had to drop out of school it would look like she couldn't afford it any longer, and that would be even worse." Amy laughed wryly.

"Sounds complicated." Luke's dad wholly supported him. He couldn't fathom what Amy described.

"That's Claire for you." She clarified, "My mom. I think it's probably a really hard way to live." Amy

shrugged again. "Anyway, I'm thinking about just not telling her. At least for now."

Luke was silent for a moment. "You know, it's none of my business, and you didn't ask me for my opinion, but if you want it…" His voice trailed off.

"I definitely want it. I thought that was the point of talking about it."

"I think you should tell her the truth." Luke took a deep breath, surprised by what he was about to share with Amy. "When I was twelve years old, I broke a window in my house because my brother and I were playing baseball in the backyard. My mom had forbidden us from playing ball in the backyard for that very reason, but one day when she wasn't home, we decided to do it anyway. So, when we ending up breaking the window, we came up with a story about some other neighborhood kids who were playing back there and that we had nothing to do with it."

Amy smiled at him. "You were just a kid. I'm sure your mother probably figured you were lying anyway. So, what happened? Did she ever find out?"

Luke paused again and took a deep breath. "Well, we never had a chance to confess. A week later my mom died in a really bad car crash on a stormy night. I feel like I've lived with that lie forever. I'd give anything to go back and tell her the truth."

Amy reached out and touched his hand. As she did, he smiled at her. She quickly pulled her hand away and stood up. "You want to grab some lunch before we run out of time?"

Luke's face lit up. "I'd love to."

***

Luke had driven the three blocks to Dawn's sorority house so many times in the last couple of years that he figured he could probably do it with his eyes closed. Tonight felt different, though, for so many reasons. He had thought more about Amy than Dawn for the last few days, and he was feeling more than a little guilty about that. He knew how much Dawn cared about him, and it killed him to think that he was thinking about another girl so often. He didn't know how things had gotten so far with his feelings for Amy, but he knew he had to do something about it. Even though nothing had happened with Amy, he couldn't help but think that he was somehow cheating on Dawn. He never really thought of himself as the cheating kind. He had been so devoted to Dawn for all this time without ever a thought for another girl. These feelings were coming from everywhere, and he had to figure out how to put an end to them.

Tonight, he and Dawn would go out and have so much fun that he would forget all about Amy. He would somehow make this up to Dawn, and she would never even have to know. As he took the front porch steps to her house two at a time, he was feeling quite optimistic again.

Dawn was waiting for him and pulled the door open just as he was about to ring the bell.

"Hello, gorgeous." Dawn pulled him close to her and gave him a long lingering kiss.

He pulled away suddenly. "Dawn, I have something to tell you."

"Okay, what is it? You look so serious." Dawn flashed him her million-dollar smile.

"I think we need to break up."

Dawn giggled and punched him on the arm. "That's really funny, Luke. Come on, what do you want to do tonight?"

"No, Dawn, I'm sorry. I'm serious. I think I'm in love with someone else." Even Dawn wasn't more stunned than he was by his own words.

***

Luke couldn't help but notice when Amy all but stopped talking to him. He shrugged it off, thinking he must have been wrong about how she felt about him, but it didn't change the way he felt about her. For weeks she had done her best to ignore him. On the night their group had finally finished their project, he and Amy were alone after Christopher and Jill had gone home. Luke nonchalantly asked Amy if she wanted to get a drink to celebrate the fact that they were done. He touched her hand slightly as it rested on the table. She jerked it away and jumped from the table saying, "No, I've got a thing." She bounced away, and that was the last time he saw her for a while.

Later, when he got home, he went up to Christopher's room. Christopher reached into his minifridge and pulled out two beers. "Can you believe we're finally finished with that stupid project? I thought we would never be done with that thing."

"What do you think about Amy?" Luke blurted out.

Christopher took a swig of his beer and shrugged. "She's pretty quiet; I don't really know that much about her. She's smart, I guess. Why?" Christopher glanced at him knowingly and raised his eyebrows slightly. "How's Dawn?"

Luke took a long swallow of his beer. "I broke up with her."

Christopher pretended to almost fall off his chair. "What? When? You guys have been together forever."

"I don't know, dude. A few weeks ago, I guess."

Christopher stared, slack jawed, at him for a minute. "You broke up with her a few weeks ago, and you're just telling me now? Why? What happened?"

Luke stared into his empty beer can. "I just didn't think it was working out."

"Why didn't you say anything?" Christopher stared at Luke for a while and waited for an answer that never came. "Wait, this doesn't have anything to do with…?"

Luke shrugged. "It doesn't matter anyway, does it? She's totally not interested. She avoids me like the plague."

"Damn, dude, she's hot and all, but she's been pretty cold lately. Maybe it's not too late to get Dawn back."

"It doesn't matter if she's into me or not. I couldn't stay with Dawn when I felt this way about someone else. It just isn't right."

"Wait a minute. Are you in love with Amy?" The realization slowly dawned on Christopher; he let out a long low whistle. "She's probably being cold because she's been thinking all this time that you have girlfriend. We all did. Are you going to tell her?"

Luke looked panicked. "No way! If she doesn't like me, it would just look desperate."

Christopher didn't say anything for a few minutes. "How did Dawn take it?"

"How do you think?"

As Luke stared at the house now that he owned with Amy, he felt a little like he did that day. He was desperately in love with her, but once again, he couldn't have her. It was such a painful feeling, unrequited love, but this time it was much worse because now she hated him, she loathed him, she wished that he didn't even exist. He put the car in gear and drove away.

***

Amy stayed in her bed until she finally heard his car pull away. *Took him long enough.* She walked into the living room and straight to the bar. She grabbed a new bottle of vodka, and as she poured herself a drink she felt tears well up in her eyes.

She tried not to think back to that time in college when they had worked on their physics project together.

By the time their group wrapped up their project, Amy had grown to really like Luke. His vulnerable side surprised her, and before she knew it, he had wriggled his way into her heart. She couldn't stop thinking about him and increasingly found herself excited to see him again. But of course, she knew it was doomed because he had a girlfriend. She was never the type to chase someone who had already made a commitment to someone else. When he'd asked her to get a drink upon the completion of their project, she'd recoiled and made up an excuse. She figured it would be too hard to be alone with him.

A week or two after their project was complete, she finally mustered up the courage to tell her mother about her English grade. The conversation went about as well as she'd expected, and she went to the bar by herself to take the edge off. As she sat staring into her drink, it wasn't long before her mind drifted to Luke. Their project turned out really great, and it was a relief to be done with it, but she also knew that the group wouldn't be spending time together and she wouldn't be seeing Luke anymore. As painful as it was to be around him, somehow she thought not being around him would be even more painful. Before long she realized she was crying.

She didn't notice that Christopher also happened to be at the same bar with some friends. He saw her and walked up behind her to put a hand on her shoulder. Startled, she jumped. When she saw that it was Christopher, embarrassment flushed her cheeks, and she wiped the tears away.

"Oh hey," she said as nonchalantly as she could.

"You okay? Do you need some company?"

Amy just shrugged it off. "It's really nothing. I'm totally fine."

Christopher shrugged back at her and turned to walk away. He paused before he turned to face her again.

"This wouldn't by any chance be about Luke, would it?" Christopher asked, trying to tread carefully.

"What are you talking about? No, of course not." Amy pretended to look surprised.

"Okay, right, well, I just thought you might want to know that Luke broke up with Dawn over a month ago, but he wasn't planning on ever telling you."

"Why would he tell me? Why would I care about that?" Amy stared into her drink, pretending not to care what Christopher would say next.

117

Christopher stared at her in amazement.

"Because he's in love with you, you idiot, and I'm pretty sure you feel the same way, but for whatever reason you two can't seem to sort this out, so now I'm stuck here playing cupid for your dumbasses instead of playing quarters with my buddies over there. Which reminds me, I have to go play quarters now. Hope you feel better." Christopher turned on his heel and walked away.

Amy started to say something but changed her mind. Christopher was already out of earshot. She flagged the bartender back over and tried to wrap her head around what Christopher had just told her. Had Luke really broken up with Dawn a month ago? Had Christopher just said that Luke was in love with her? This must be some kind of a stupid joke. She supposed it made sense that Luke didn't want to tell her. She'd been pretty obnoxious around him lately. She ordered another drink and pondered what to do. It didn't take her long.

Chapter 6

As Brianna sat on the bathroom floor, she stared at herself in the full-length mirror on the back of the door and tried to catch her breath. She couldn't understand exactly why she had done it again. She knew it would be more difficult to hide the scars that were multiplying on her thighs. This time would be the last time. Never again. Sometimes it seemed as if cutting herself was out of her own control. She'd begged herself to stop, even as she was doing it, but it was a different force that took over. She looked down at the razor blade shaking in her hand, now crimson with her blood. Tears spilled down her cheeks as she watched her thighs bleed from the fresh cuts she had made into each of them. One in each thigh. Another matching set. As she watched the blood ooze from the lacerations on her legs, she began to feel cathartic, both horrified and ecstatic. More tears fell, and she dropped the razor into the tub. She held her head in her hands and sobbed. *Why? Why?*

***

Jack hadn't moved much in a few days. Justin called a few times, begging him to please come in and have the body scan. Jack needed to start the chemo and not wait any longer, Justin's messages urged. Time was now of the essence.

A couple of days ago, Jack felt his last pangs of hunger. Those were completely gone now. Besides, food would just delay the inevitable. The water bottle by his bed was long empty and he stared longingly at it. His parched body wanted more, but pain and exhaustion kept him from doing anything about it. Besides, he knew dehydration would help speed up his death.

Inhale. Exhale. The sound of his breath was his only comfort these days and other times it was the bane of his existence. As long as he was breathing, it meant he was still alive. He drifted into a dream.

Jack stood on the bridge, clutching Melissa's balloons. Just as he was readying himself to release them, he thought he saw something move in the corner of his eye. He looked to his left and saw a boy who looked to be a young teenager. He was holding something in his hands. Jack moved closer to the boy and saw that he was holding a scarf. The scarf was unusual, unlike anything Jack had ever seen. It was made of satin, and silver in color, but when the moonlight shone on it, a pink thread that ran through it was revealed. As Jack moved still closer to the boy, drawn to the scarf, he noticed that it also had pink doves embroidered on it.

The boy looked at Jack as he approached. Jack thought he saw the boy smile, and he was about to ask what he was doing there when the boy said "Catch." The boy threw one end of the scarf to Jack and then leapt off the side of the bridge. Gasping, Jack released the balloons as he grabbed the scarf in one miraculous movement. He gripped it with all of his strength, holding the weight of the boy as he dangled from the other end of the scarf, hovering above certain death. The menacing water lurched below the boy as the peaceful creek became a vast dark ocean with strong undertows. The muscles in Jack's arm stretched as he clung to the scarf, desperate to save the boy's life. "Hold on!" He used every bit of strength to pull the boy back up. The boy simply gave him a peaceful, yet understanding, smile. Horrified, Jack watched the boy let go and plummet to the watery depths below.

Jack leaned as far over the bridge as he could, panting. He screamed for the boy, but he heard and saw nothing after the splash. He looked at his hands and noticed that he was still holding the scarf.

Jack awoke, the terror of the dream lingering. The image of the scarf was burned into his brain. He looked down and saw that he was clutching the blankets in his hands as he had been clutching the scarf in his dream. He'd been a doctor long enough to have heard about these kinds of things. It wasn't too unusual to dream of death when you were dying. But he couldn't think about that now; he needed something to distract him from the horror. He tried to shake off the feeling as he picked up the remote and flipped on the TV. Some guy on public television shouted about the importance of living your dream and your passion. This guy seemed to think that purchasing his software and his book would instantly transform your life. Jack smirked. *What could this guy do for me?*

Strangely, he found himself thinking back to a time in high school when he had taken piano lessons. His teacher seemed to think that he had profound potential as a musician and pianist. He remembered being very proud of his work and accomplishments in that class and had considered studying piano in college. His mentor had encouraged him to apply to Juilliard to become classically trained. Of course, his mother wouldn't stand for it. Artistry was only for weak people; he needed a strong career, like a surgeon. That was the last time he ever thought about having a career in art and music. Somehow, the shouting guy on the television had dredged up a long-lost dream. Maybe this guy was on to something. He smirked again and changed the channel to sports news.

***

Luke let himself into his hotel room and looked around. There was nothing in the drab room to make it feel like home except a couple of pictures of Jonathan and Amy that he put near the bed when he had moved in. He picked up the photo of Jonathan and touched the glass that covered his face. He set it back down and lifted up the picture of Amy. He gazed at it with tears in his eyes. So quickly he lost everything that mattered to him. In the blink of an eye, it was all gone. *How had it happened like that? What had I done to deserve that? Maybe Amy was right. This was my fault; I created this whole mess.* But it certainly wasn't what he wanted. He wanted everything to go back to the way it was. He wanted his family back, his beautiful son and the woman of his dreams. This was not the way it was supposed to end. Not when it had started with such a fairy tale beginning. When people had nightmares like this, they were supposed to wake up. But not him, not this nightmare. Every night, he went to sleep thinking that when he woke up the dream would finally be over, but instead it just kept going. Day after dreaded day, he awoke to the same damned thing. He tried to pull his head above the raging waters and swim to shore, but the tides kept pulling him under and wouldn't let him escape. He could see no way out.

To add insult to injury, he was starting to get the message that Amy was never going to talk to him again. He had held out hope for a long time that she would eventually come around, but as the weeks ticked by into a month, he doubted that it would ever happen. He didn't know how he was going to get through all of this without her. The memories of their blissful beginning plagued him.

Luke was playing foosball in the living room of his frat house. It was turning out to be a pretty intense game, which matched his mood lately. He didn't even glance up from the table when the doorbell rang, completely oblivious to whether or not anyone had even bothered to answer the door. His goalie had just blocked a close one, and he couldn't afford to lose his concentration now.

"Yo, Luke," Simon shouted into the living room. "Visitor."

Luke let a goal slip past him. "Shit." He looked up at Peter who was smirking at him. 9-9. "I'll be right back. This is not over yet." Luke pushed the table angrily and headed for the front door. He stopped in his tracks when he saw her standing in the doorway. What was she doing here? He looked down at his beer stained sweatshirt. He was pretty sure he hadn't showered in a day or so.

He tried to look casual. "Hey."

Amy smiled shyly at him. "Can I talk to you for a second?"

"Sure." Luke stepped out onto the porch. "Do you want to sit?" He pointed to a bench near the door.

"No, that's okay. I can't stay."

Luke noticed that she was standing unconventionally close to him. He felt like his lungs might explode, so he tried to control his breathing. She stood close enough that he thought maybe he could feel her breath as she looked up at him. His heart raced, and heat rushed to his face and neck. He waited patiently for her to explain why she was there, but she was taking an awfully long time to get to her point. Not that he minded if she never got to it; he could have stayed on that porch with her all night. He felt her take a step back.

"I just wondered if you heard yet if the grades came out for the physics project. I heard from someone else in the class…" She drifted off and glanced away. They both looked into the open window of the frat house as UB40 crooned "Red Red Wine."

Luke looked down at his feet. "No, I haven't heard anything yet, but if I do, I can definitely call you."

"Yeah, okay, thanks. I was just wondering." Amy turned to leave, but she was still on the porch.

Luke ached for her to stay, but he couldn't think of a reason to convince her to. She took a few more steps then stopped, and his heart did too. She turned to look at him. "Luke?"

"Yes?"

"Did you break up with Dawn?"

His breath caught in his throat. How did she know that? "Yes," he said hoarsely.

She audibly inhaled sharply as though she had been holding her breath too. They stared at each other for what seemed an eternity. Finally, before he even realized what he was doing, he stepped next to her and touched her face. UB40 was still playing as they kissed for the first time.

He went cautiously at first, but it took a lot of self-restraint. It wasn't long before she was kissing him back, and they stayed locked in their embrace ever since.

And there they had stayed, through many years, until that painfully fateful day when they lost Jonathan, and he lost everything.

***

"Catch."

Again, the boy threw the scarf to him, and Jack scrambled for it just in time as the boy leapt over the side of the bridge. He stared up at Jack and seemed calm as he dangled above the icy water.

"Hold on!" Jack screamed at the boy.

Jack could feel his feet slip from beneath him as the weight of the boy seemed to increase. He held on with all of his strength, but his feet were slipping more now, and he felt he would lose his balance. He could feel his muscles contracting and aching as he tried to hold the weight of the boy. Terrified he would fall off the bridge, in a snap decision Jack let go of the scarf. He leaned over the rail of the bridge as he watched the boy plunge into the water. Jack screamed and sobbed into his hands.

He awoke with tears on his face. Jack tried to shake off the feeling of the dream, but it was too powerful to let go. He struggled to get out of bed, but he needed a distraction. He checked his cell phone for messages; there were fifteen from Justin. Jack picked up the phone and called him back. Justin wasn't going to leave him alone until he called back anyway.

"I was afraid I wasn't going to hear from you." Justin answered on the first ring. "I really think you need an evaluation."

"When can I come in?" Jack asked nonchalantly.

"What are you doing now?"

"Well, let me check my schedule." Jack grunted sarcastically.

Ninety minutes later Jack, Justin, and Harold from Oncology were discussing his treatment options. The cancer had spread to his lungs, just as Jack thought, so they agreed the prognosis was not good. However, with treatment, he could probably extend his life for a few more months at least. *But what would be the point?*

"How about taking a walk outside? Some fresh air could do both of us some good. I've been holed up in this hospital since last night."

"Sure, I could probably use some air too." Ironically, Jack was actually feeling agreeable for the first time in weeks.

***

As Nancy sat in Amy's house again – staring her down – Amy could feel herself losing her patience. Apparently, the drunken fit of rage directed at her sister hadn't been enough to set her off course. Amy had agreed to take a shower that morning, thinking that it would make Nancy happy enough to go away, but no such luck. Nancy wasn't going anywhere, and somehow, she got it into her head that Amy was going to come with her to get a cup of coffee.

"Come on, Amy. When was the last time you left this house?"

"Jonathan's funeral, not that it's any of your business." Amy snapped at her sister.

"Amy, that was over a month ago. You have to get out of this house. You're just dying a slow death in here. Please." Nancy begged.

Amy was more annoyed than ever. She couldn't figure out why her sister was so interested in her all of a sudden. She had to come up with a way to get rid of her. "If I agree to have coffee with you, will you please leave me alone forever?"

Nancy sighed. This was going to be much harder than she had even anticipated. Admittedly, she had not been the greatest sister in the past, but she knew how much her sister needed her now and felt that she should try to make up for it as much as possible.

She also knew that her sister was more than a little angry with her for never keeping in touch. Even after Jonathan was born, Nancy found it really difficult to stay connected to her sister and nephew. She preferred to watch from afar. She was happy just knowing that they were happy. Amy had expressed her disappointment with Nancy on more than one occasion for not trying harder to make time for her nephew.

Nancy suspected, now that Jonathan was gone, it was probably in the forefront of Amy's mind how she had just squandered away all the time she could have spent with Jonathan that now she could never recover.

Of course, Nancy agreed, but she wasn't able to fully understand why she was never able to make a connection with them. It seemed like her whole life she was battling this same losing fight. She couldn't say for sure just how many friends she had lost in her lifetime due to her lack of keeping in touch. She saw groups of girlfriends in restaurants and out shopping and often wondered why she never had that. Deep down, she recognized it was her lack of effort that eventually got her squeezed out of a group of friends. Even the few remaining friends that were still hanging around, due to their undying loyalty, knew that the friendship was just limping along.

As for boyfriends, her track record was not much better. Any time she ever got close to a man, she would suddenly start finding things wrong with him or find a way to sabotage their relationship.

She was never able to really understand why she wasn't like other people. She'd spent most of her life feeling weird and defective. This time was no exception. She not only had alienated her sister, she had also managed to alienate her nephew, with whom she would never have another chance.

"Fine, if you come with me to coffee, I will wait two weeks before I come back to check on you. The only condition is you have to promise me you won't drink."

Amy weighed the options in her mind. Two whole weeks of peace sounded like a good deal. Although, the not drinking part sounded excruciating, the thought of being left alone far outweighed it. She could just grab a cup of coffee and be on her way; Nancy never said how long she had to be out.

"Fine," Amy picked up her coat and headed toward the door. A surprising light snow was falling, and she opened her closet to reach for a hat and scarf. "It must be colder outside than I thought."

Nancy was so pleasantly surprised by the fact that Amy agreed to come, she was practically skipping by the time they got outside. Amy glared at her as she walked alongside her.

"Doesn't it feel good to get out of the house?"

Amy did actually think the unseasonably cold October air felt somewhat refreshing, but she would never give her sister the satisfaction. She chose instead to just ignore the question.

Amy's brownstone home was only a few quick blocks to the coffee shop, so the walk was easy. Something about the brisk air was making Amy feel better, and her mind felt a little sharper than it had in a long time.

Nancy gestured at Amy's scarf. "That's really pretty. Where did it come from?"

She touched the silver satin and gazed at the delicate pink doves. "Luke's grandmother made it. The whole thing is handmade. It's my favorite, not just because it's so pretty, but because there's not another one like it on the planet."

"She's really talented. I hadn't realized. How can I get her to make me one too?"

Amy rolled her eyes at Nancy as they stopped to let two gentlemen pass before opening the door to the coffee shop.

Jack and Justin strolled by the coffee shop across the street from the hospital and nodded to the women who were kind enough to let them pass on the sidewalk. Jack stopped dead in his tracks.

"Are you alright? Are you feeling okay?" Justin was concerned.

Jack could barely speak when he saw the red-haired woman's scarf. He recognized it immediately as the scarf from the dream, but he had no idea how to begin to explain that to Justin.

"Jack? Are you okay?" Justin took his arm.

"Uh, yeah, I'm fine. You want to go in here and sit down?" Jack motioned toward the coffee shop door.

"Sure. Maybe this walk was too much for you." Justin opened the door and helped Jack inside.

Jack scanned the room, looking for the woman with the scarf. He spotted her at a table by the corner. The blonde woman she came in with was standing at the counter talking to the person behind it. Jack made his way through the room and found a table near theirs. As he sat down, his gaze momentarily connected with the red-haired woman before he quickly looked away.

This is crazy! Those scarves are probably everywhere. He'd probably seen Amanda in one and, somehow, it translated into his dreams about that boy. Suddenly, he changed his mind; he wanted to get out of there. How could he do that without Justin thinking he'd completely lost his mind?

Justin followed him to the table. "Do you want something to drink?"

Jack shook his head a little. "Maybe just some water." His gaze followed the other woman, the blonde, as she brought two steaming cups of coffee over to the woman with the scarf. He then watched as Justin put in his order.

"That coffee is in a mug," the redhead stated, frowning at the blond.

"Uh, yeah, that's the traditional way to serve coffee," the blonde quipped back.

"But I don't want to sit here to drink it; I want to go."

"No, you said you would get coffee with me." Irritation crept into the blonde's voice.

Jack discreetly listened to the women argue.

"And I have, so let's go." The woman with the scarf started to stand up.

Her companion pushed her back down in her seat. "The deal was coffee, and then I'd stay away for two weeks. I swear to God, Amy, if you don't drink every sip of that coffee, I will stalk you every day for the next month."

Jack raised his eyebrows at the details of their conversation.

Justin returned and placed a cup of water in front of Jack. He picked it up and started to take a few swallows.

"I don't have to listen to you." The woman with the scarf, who he now knew was Amy, was pouting, but she was drinking her coffee.

"I am trying to help you. I just don't know how." The other woman's eyes welled up with tears.

"Well, I don't want your help. And what are you crying about? You're not the one whose fifteen-year-old son drowned." Amy spit the words out through clenched teeth.

Jack spit his water out so hard it hit Justin squarely in the face. Stunned, his friend picked up a napkin and mopped up his glasses. "What the hell, Jack?"

The blonde woman didn't know what to say. Jack didn't know what to say. Both tables sat in silence. The minutes dragged on. Justin continued to stare at Jack, hoping for an explanation.

Amy looked into her cup; from the angle, Jack saw it was half gone. "Can I go now?"

The blonde just shrugged. "Come on, let's go."

The women stood up to leave. Jack's gaze followed them out the door.

"Ready?" He asked Justin.

"Sure." Justin looked perplexed. "*What* is going on?"

Jack stared at his friend for a second. "Probably nothing; let's get going on that walk now. I'm feeling much stronger."

They went outside, and they overheard the blonde woman telling Amy that she'd walk her home, and then she would leave her alone.

"Fine," Amy agreed, "but I'm only letting you because it's such a short walk."

Jack knew it was probably a bad idea, but he trailed after them. His back pain seemed to have subsided somewhat, so he and Justin walked silently side by side for the three blocks to Amy's home. Jack, from the other side of the street, watched her unlock her front door and let herself in.

"Do you know her or something?" Justin was still somewhat perplexed.

"I don't think so." Jack stared at her front door for a second, and the two of them turned back toward the hospital.

***

Jack stared at the hospital ceiling from his bed after he'd finished his first round of chemotherapy. Justin had urged him to stay in the hospital for a while so he could monitor his reaction to the treatment. So far, Jack didn't really feel much of anything, except extreme fatigue. As he stared at the holes in the acoustic ceiling tiles, he began to realize how alone he was in the world. *Will anyone at all miss me when I'm gone?* He imagined the world without him in it and, depressingly, it looked exactly the same. *What have I ever made of my life? What difference have I made? What legacy will I leave behind? I have nothing to show for this life at all.* He had acquired a lot of money and lived like a king in a big house. It all amounted to nothing. He counted up the years and cursed every one of them.

He hated himself. The inner critic settled in around him like an uninvited houseguest. *You are useless. You are a wimp. You have not amounted to anything.* The recordings replayed over and over again through his mind. He squeezed his eyes closed and covered his ears, trying to block out the incoming messages. He rolled onto his side and blinked away his tears. *You're a crybaby too.*

His thoughts drifted to the woman in the coffee shop. He had read about strange things happening to people through ESP and intuition, but what happened to him must have been just a bizarre coincidence. His thoughts turned to synchronicity and angels, but he quickly dismissed it. He didn't believe in any of those things. Besides, he was way too tired from the chemo to be thinking clearly now, anyway. His eyelids got heavier and heavier.

Jack and the boy stood looking at each other on the bridge in a kind of show down. "You're not jumping off this time." Jack yelled at the boy.

"Catch."

The boy smiled and threw him one end of the scarf. "No, no, no, no, no." Jack cried out as he grabbed the scarf and helplessly watched the boy do his usual catapult over the side of the bridge. He knew he could not let go this time; he had to figure out how to save this boy from falling into the water. He wouldn't just allow him to kill himself. As Jack secured his feet against the edge of the bridge, he held on as tightly as he could. He screamed at the boy to hold on. "Please don't let go. Please don't let go. I'm going to help you this time."

Once again, the boy let go, and Jack watched him plunge fatally into the water. "NO!" Jack screamed. He ripped his coat and shoes off and dove head first into the water after the boy. As his body hit the water, instead of the icy pain that he had braced himself for, everything seemed calm and serene. The boy swam up to him and smiled. Soft music filled his ears. The boy was swimming effortlessly around him like a dolphin. He was peaceful and at ease.

"Tell my mom I can swim as much as I want here. Tell her she doesn't have to worry about me anymore."

Jack opened his eyes and stared at the holes in the ceiling tiles again. He had goosebumps and remembered the dream. He slowly sat up in bed and rubbed his face. *I don't want to remember. I want to forget.* He got out of the hospital bed and shook off the remnants of the dream. He had too much on his mind today to get caught up in the memories of the nightmare.

He had some preparation to do today because tomorrow he would make his official retirement announcement. But for now, he just wanted to go home and get into his own bed. He didn't want to think about retirement yet. He had so many other plans for himself and for his career. It was hard to believe that everything was being cut short and taken from him. He felt cheated, but there wasn't anything he could do about it. He gave the hospital bed a good punch before exiting the room.

***

Amy sat down in the living room and stared at the bar. She'd promised Nancy she wouldn't drink for at least the two weeks of space that she was giving her. *I don't want a drink anyway.* The fresh air from walking home gave her a little bit of energy, and she actually felt like doing something. She wandered around the house for a while and found herself in the bedroom. She looked at her bed and the sheets that she hadn't changed since Jonathan died. She started stripping the bed of its clothes and carried them into the laundry room. She shoved everything into the washing machine and sat down on the floor to watch the sheets dance around and around each other in the washer. It reminded her of a time when she and Luke used to love to dance.

One afternoon, when Jonathan was ten years old, Luke had been spinning her around and around the kitchen with "Red Red Wine" playing on the radio. They were smiling at each other, both of them transported back to the night of their first kiss when the song had been blaring from the windows of Luke's fraternity house. Swiftly, Amy found Luke's gentle mouth on hers as he attempted a replay of that night.

"What are you doing?"

They'd heard Jonathan's voice and knew the moment was gone. They'd looked at each other and laughed, expecting to see a horrified Jonathan for having witnessed their little make-out session in the kitchen. Instead, he seemed more aghast by the music they were listening to.

"What is this music?"

"This song reminds us of our college days, when we first met." Luke had taken Amy into his arms and spun her around again before dipping her.

"You guys are so old." Jonathan rolled his eyes and left the room. She and Luke burst out laughing again.

Now, as the washing machine's buzzer pulled her back into the present reality, the memory struck her over the head like a lead pipe, and she burst into tears.

Chapter 7

Brianna let herself into the apartment after school. It was silent, but what else was new? She was accustomed to being home alone. She used to look forward to the time right before bed when she and her dad would catch up on their days, but he'd recently picked up another job. He was working at the drug store now, which meant that he came home long after she had gone to bed. She had come to cherish the little talks they would have right before she went to sleep, but now even that was gone. *Quit feeling sorry for yourself. Dad sacrifices a lot for me.*

She went into her dad's room and opened his closet door. She felt bad about how she'd treated him the last time they saw each other and hoped she could make it up to him. She found what she was looking for in a box inside, dragged it out, and opened it. Inside, she found paints, watercolors, brushes, and rolled up canvases. These things used to make her dad so happy. Maybe they still would. She laid everything out for him in his bedroom and hoped it would work…if he found the time.

As she wandered into the living room, trying to find another excuse not to do her homework, her mind drifted to Mark. Luckily, her friends hadn't made a big deal about her fainting at Erin's house the other night. Erin told her that she had only passed out for a few seconds. Worried, Erin had really wanted to go in the house and tell her parents, but Brianna had already been too humiliated because it had happened in front of Mark again. She'd begged Erin not to tell her parents, and Erin had reluctantly agreed.

She turned the television on, and her stomach growled. Lunch was a lifetime ago. She walked into the kitchen and yanked open the refrigerator.

She pulled the peanut butter and jelly out and found a few pieces of bread still in the cupboard. Even though they were just the end pieces, having bread in there was a stroke of luck. Sometimes, for dinner she would just eat the peanut butter and jelly right from the jar with a spoon. She generously spread the condiments on her bread and headed back to the television. As she did, she felt a little dizziness, and black spots began to fill her vision. She felt like she was going to throw up right before the room started to spin…

Brianna awoke on the living room floor and blinked a few times, trying to figure out where she was. *How did I get here?* Her head throbbed. She stood up and saw the peanut butter and jelly sandwich on the floor. *Oh, right. I was making myself dinner. I must have fainted again.*

She put her hand up to her forehead and felt something wet. Her fingers came away bloody. She ran to look in a mirror and saw that she was bleeding quite a bit. The hospital was only a few blocks away. She could walk.

***

Lawrence panicked as he ran down the street toward the hospital. He figured he'd be fired again because his manager at the drug store hadn't looked too impressed when he told him he had to go to his daughter in the emergency room. He ran through the doors of the hospital and scanned the waiting room. He spotted her sitting by herself in a chair in the corner.

"Brianna!" Lawrence shouted.

Brianna jumped up and ran into his arms. Lawrence brushed back her bangs to see the bandage covering the stitches in her forehead.

"Oh, my poor baby," Lawrence started to cry. "I'm so sorry I wasn't there."

Brianna just laughed. "It wasn't a big deal, Dad. I knew what to do. I'm just really glad you're here now."

Lawrence sighed. This was not how this was supposed to be. He was supposed to be taking care of his daughter. He held her tightly in his arms, wishing he never had to let her go. As he held her to him, a doctor approached.

"Is this your dad?" The doctor addressed Brianna.

"Yep, this is him." Brianna gave him another squeeze.

"She hit her head pretty hard. I don't see any signs of a concussion, but I'd like you to keep an eye on her. If she seems confused at all, or if she vomits, I need you to bring her back in here."

"Sure thing, Doc. Thanks for taking care of her. Where do we check out?" Lawrence turned to a woman sitting behind the desk.

The doctor put her hand on his arm. "Not so fast. Brianna also told me about the fainting spells that she's been having. That could really be the sign of something more serious. I'd like to do a CAT scan."

"Oh no, I really can't afford that at this time." Lawrence grimaced.

"Okay, but don't risk this. Take her to see her doctor as soon as you can."

As Lawrence and Brianna walked silently home together, he was pulled back to a time when he was just a kid about Brianna's age. He remembered how scared he had been when he fell off his bike and broke his arm. There had been no one to help him either, and he'd walked to the hospital all by himself too. The only difference was, there was no one to pick him up, and he had to walk home with his newly casted arm by himself. He had made up some lie about his father waiting for him in the parking lot, but he had a feeling they knew he had been lying. *Why can't I take better care of Brianna than my father did me?*

When Brianna was born, he vowed that things would be different for her. He thought she would never have to go through the hardships he had endured as a young boy with no mother and an alcoholic father. He was going to spoil this child and give her the world if that's what she wanted. He didn't know how he would provide for her, but he was going to figure it out. He was really going to make something of himself. He would run an art gallery or, better yet, own his own gallery. He'd really be a part of something that would dazzle the world.

He had always loved painting. In high school, his art teacher had told him that she had never seen art like his at the high school level. She wanted him to pursue a career in painting, but his father made damn sure he knew where he stood on that idea by belittling it to death and after Brianna was born that really no longer seemed like an option for him anyway. He had to get to work to start providing for his baby. He couldn't just waste time painting all day, hoping that someone, somewhere might be interested in what he was doing. Now, he couldn't remember the last time he held a paintbrush.

As he walked his baby girl home from the hospital, he had to face that he was just as big a failure as his father had been. *What have I ever done to fulfill any of the promises I made to myself regarding Brianna? Where has my life gone, and is Brianna going to end up the same as me?* The thought terrified him. There had to be another way. He took Brianna's hand in his and gave it a little squeeze. She beamed back at him.

She was so sweet. Despite everything, she still managed to be easygoing and happy. She never really asked much of him. It almost made him feel more like a failure because it was as if she knew not to expect any more. In fact, she'd been so quiet lately that he didn't even know what she had been up to these days. They used to talk all the time, but he knew they were becoming more and more distant because he was spending less and less time at home with her. He knew he was to blame. But how in the world was he going to dig his way out of this situation? He was damned if he did and damned if he didn't.

They let themselves into their apartment; the situation weighing heavy in his heart. After he tucked her into bed, he went to his own room, exhausted from all the events of the day. That's when he saw the canvas and paints all set up and ready for him to use.

***

Jack finished several more rounds of chemotherapy over the next weeks. Other than the overwhelming fatigue and wavering appetite, he wasn't feeling all that bad. On the days that he had his appetite back, he even managed to go for a few drives around town. The motivation to get out was largely driven by his compulsion to see the scarf woman again. He couldn't explain why, but he had driven past her brownstone several times. He felt drawn to her and felt a need to be close to her even if he couldn't see her. The thought crossed his mind to drive by her house today, but his exhaustion took over. He was too tired to even get out of bed. His battle-worn body wouldn't allow it. He quickly drifted to sleep; as usual, the sleep was fitful.

Exhausted moments of wakefulness were interrupted by long, extended periods of horrific nightmares. His dreams had been hijacked by his enraged mother. At times, even when he thought he was awake, a vision of his mother would appear. The line between wakefulness and sleep was disappearing.

She was screaming at him and banging on the wall with what looked like a hammer. Isadora was calling to him from behind a door; he pulled and pulled trying to open the door but it wouldn't budge. Melissa was crawling on the floor, coughing and choking on blood. He tried to help her to her feet, but they both slipped on her blood and fell.

He slept on and off, soaking the sheets with his sweat. He tossed and turned in a wet tangled mess. Plagued with the sudden horror that this is what the rest of his short life would be, he groaned in frustration and pain.

He was underwater again with the boy. The boy swam up to him and gave him a dazzling smile. "You didn't tell her yet."

Jack looked at the boy and realized that he too could talk underwater. Or maybe they were communicating in a different way. "I don't know what you mean."

"Yes, do you. You go to her house sometimes. Tell her. Tell her I'm happy and I can swim all the time without anyone having to worry. It doesn't even have to be summer for me to swim here. I'm safe now. Tell her. My name is Jonathan."

Out of nowhere, a beautiful young girl swam up to Jonathan and took his hand. She was shimmering in the water, and Jack noted that she wore a pink shirt with purple butterflies. The girl began to pull Jonathan away from Jack. "Come on Jonathan; it's time to go now."

In the distance, behind the kids, he thought for a fleeting moment that he saw Melissa.

Jack awoke with a start, frustrated that he couldn't just rest. The torture of the nightmares once again forced him from his bed. He fought his way out of the tangled mess of sheets and blankets like a child having a tantrum. He pulled on his clothing that was strewn haphazardly on the floor. He didn't know exactly what he would do, but he was not going to stay here.

He found himself driving by the hospital and ultimately pulling onto her street. He nervously pulled his car up to the curb across from her house. Hours went by as he watched, waiting for any kind of movement. Another two hours went by. *This is crazy. What am I doing here? What are the odds of her son's name being Jonathan anyway? That couldn't possibly be his name.* He just couldn't shake the feeling that it might be. *But then what? What if his name really was Jonathan? Then what?*

He shrugged, unsure what to do, and drove home. Over the next several days he felt compelled to drive to her house to see if she would come out. She never did. By the fourth day, Jack got out of his car. *What am I doing? I'm not going to knock on the door. That would be crazy. I'm just going to stretch my legs.* As he stood up, he felt the earth spin beneath him. He remembered it had been a whole day since he'd last had anything to eat; his appetite had disappeared again. Weakness settled into his legs, and he felt them buckle beneath him. He grabbed the door of his car to keep from falling.

"You okay, Mister?"

Jack snapped his head up and saw the blonde woman from the coffee shop. She'd caught him so completely off guard that he had no idea how to respond to her. He'd never actually considered what he would say if he ever had a chance to talk to either of these women.

"Ah yeah, there's just a slick spot here. I just lost my footing. Thanks." Jack ducked back into his car and drove off as quickly as he could.

***

Amy opened the door and let Nancy into the house.

"Well, isn't this a surprise? You are actually opening the door for me?"

Amy smiled. "Don't get used to it. I guess I'm just feeling generous today."

Nancy was pleased. It seemed that in the last couple of weeks, Amy had started to perk up even if it was in the tiniest ways. She was much easier to talk to these days and even looked like she had probably washed her hair recently. Maybe today Nancy would even be able to convince her to eat something.

On that note, Nancy strolled into the kitchen and opened the refrigerator. She began pulling things out. "What would you say to a grilled cheese with bacon? That sounds great, doesn't it?"

Amy shrugged. Eating still didn't tempt her, but she figured maybe it sounded a little bit like a good idea. Her sister knew that had always been her favorite sandwich since as far back as either of them could remember. Even though they weren't particularly close as children, or as adults for that matter, Nancy still managed to know almost everything there was to know about Amy.

She busily piled the sandwich high with cheese and watched the bacon sizzle in the pan for a while. Amy walked over and stood next to her in front of the stove. They watched the sandwich in silence.

"It's just not fair," Amy blurted out.

"I know it's not. It's not at all." Nancy flipped the sandwich over.

"No, that's not what I mean; it's just not fair how it happened. Ever since they diagnosed him with epilepsy, I took every precaution, I never missed giving him his medication, and I never left him alone. None of this would have happened if I hadn't left him with Luke. Luke did it on purpose. He needed so badly to prove me wrong."

Nancy put the sandwich on a plate and turned the stove off. "Honey, I really don't see it that way. He was looking at it through a different lens. He knew that Jonathan was getting older; he was fifteen years old. He also knew that Jonathan was getting frustrated with being watched all the time. He needed to have some independence. Luke was trying to let his son have some of that so that he would know what it felt like to be independent. He never would have known that Jonathan would go swimming that day. He was coming from a good place, Amy. Deep down, I'm sure you know that."

"What I know is that I was paralyzed with the fear of not being able to help my son, so I did everything I could, just to have Luke steal away what little I had. Mothers are supposed to protect their children. Luke took all that power away from me."

Nancy handed Amy the plate, looking shocked when Amy accepted it. She took a big bite of the sandwich. "This is *so* good."

As Amy thoughtfully chewed on her sandwich, she watched Nancy clean the pan at the sink.

"Hey, Nancy?"

Nancy turned off the water and looked at Amy.

"Why don't you have a boyfriend?"

Nancy dried her hands on a towel deliberately before answering. "I don't know. I guess I've just been too busy."

"But lots of women have careers and have been able to also maintain a relationship and sometimes, gasp, even start a family."

Nancy sat down next to her sister at the table. "I'm definitely not interested in starting a family."

Amy set her sandwich down. "Why is that?"

"Well, I don't know. I guess I just never really wanted to. Our parents were pretty deranged most of the time, and I guess I just wouldn't want my kids growing up in the same environment that I did."

Amy didn't say anything and picked up her sandwich again.

Nancy stood up and walked back to the sink to resume the dishes. "I really just don't want to be like Mom. I don't ever want to find out for sure that I'm emotionally unavailable. Mom squashed my hopes and dreams before I ever knew what they were. I couldn't possibly do that to my children and be able to live with myself."

***

Mark and Brianna walked hand in hand in silence all the way to her apartment.

"Thanks for walking me home." Brianna smiled at him shyly.

"No problem." Mark glanced toward Brianna's apartment building. "Are you sure you're going to be okay? Is your dad home?"

Brianna followed his glance toward the building and shrugged. "Probably not. He's not home that much."

Mark reached up and touched the bandage that covered the stitches on her head. "Do you have a neighbor or someone who can keep an eye on you? You probably shouldn't be alone."

Brianna was touched by his gesture. She knew there was no one, and she just shrugged.

Mark put his arms around her waist. "What if something happens to you again? I wouldn't be able to forgive myself. Let me just come up for a little bit to make sure you're okay."

Brianna gleefully agreed and they walked up the four flights together. She hoped that her necessitous apartment wouldn't betray her, but she knew she couldn't hide forever. She held her breath as she let him in the front door. If he noticed anything about the apartment, he didn't say anything.

Mark flopped down on the couch and turned the television on. "Your dad works a lot, doesn't he?"

Brianna ran into the kitchen, praying there was something in there to offer him. She was thrilled that there was still a little orange juice left, and she poured him a glass. She answered him from the kitchen so he wouldn't be able to see her face.

"Uh, yeah, but just because he likes to stay busy. The great part about him working so much is that we always have extra money to do what we want." She found him lounging on the couch when she came in with the orange juice. She set it on the table in front of him.

"Come sit by me." Mark patted the couch next to him.

Brianna bounced down next to him and turned her attention toward the television. "What are you watching?" Before she knew it, Mark had his mouth on hers again, and she could feel his tongue prying her mouth open. She couldn't tell if she was elated or repulsed. She thought maybe she liked it a little, but the kiss was pretty wet, and he was getting saliva all over her face. She tried to kiss him back, but his kiss was so urgent there really wasn't much room for her to do much of anything. Eventually she just gave up trying and sat frozen with her mouth open.

After a few minutes, Mark finally stopped. He touched the stitches on her head again and said, "I love you."

Happiness bubbled through her. "I love you too."

***

Amy was gaining back a little strength. Thrilled to see her sister eating again, Nancy had stopped by almost every day that week to cook for her. Even more surprisingly, Amy hadn't even complained about it. In fact, she'd actually been looking forward to seeing her sister all day.

The phone rang and Amy picked it up on the first ring. "Hello?"

"Hey, it's Nancy. I'm not going to be able to cook today; something came up at work, and

I'm going to have to be here late. I'll still stop by later though."

"It's okay, Nancy. You don't have to cook every day. I'm okay. I'll make my own food today. I haven't forgotten how." Amy laughed but couldn't help feeling a little disappointed. "Good luck with work."

Peering into her refrigerator, nothing appealed to her. She looked around at the food a minute longer and decided on Chinese takeout. There was a place a few blocks from her home that she used to love. The more she thought about it, the better it sounded. Besides, some fresh air would probably do her good anyway. With that, she pulled on her boots and coat, grabbed her purse, and headed out the door.

At first, Jack thought he was imagining that the front door was opening. He had stared so long at that door, for so many hours and days, that he thought his eyes were playing tricks on him. Sure enough, the woman with the scarf was coming out of the front door. Paralyzed with indecision, he watched her walk down the street and paused another minute before getting out of his car. He got in step behind her and began to trail her.

He followed her for three blocks and into a Chinese restaurant. He stood silently behind her in line and listened as she placed her order. Jack's stomach revolted against the idea of Chinese food, but when it was his turn, he placed an order.

Amy had taken a seat near the door and stared at a small television as she waited for her order. Jack took a seat next to hers and affixed his eyes on the television too. A weather man was droning on.

A minute later he cleared his throat. "Think we're going to get more snow soon?"

Amy started and did a slight double-take. "Are you talking to me?" She glanced over at him.

Jack smiled at her. "I guess so. I was trying to pass the time while we waited for our food."

Amy smiled back a little. "I'm not sure. I hadn't really been paying attention to the reports. I kind of like the snow though, so I'm not complaining."

Amy's name was called and she hurriedly went to the counter to pick up her order.

Jack desperately wanted her to stay; he felt compelled to get her attention again. He came to her side at the counter with his wallet in his hand. "Can I buy that for you?"

Amy looked at him strangely. "Uh, no thanks; I'm not interested."

Jack winced. *What did I think she was going to say?*

Amy paid for her order and moved as quickly toward the door as she could. Jack didn't wait for his order, but followed her out into the street. Amy started to pick up her pace, scared now. "Please get away from me." People on the sidewalk began to notice them.

"Please, I just need to talk to you." Jack watched her run away from him. *She can't get away!* "It's about Jonathan!" Her wonton soup crashed to the sidewalk as she turned back to face him in shock. The name clearly meant something to her.

"What about him? Who are you? What do you want?" Amy's voice wavered, trembling with fear.

Jack hadn't prepared himself to blurt it out like that, but he had to stop her, had to get her to listen. Now he was unsure what to say. "Can we please sit down somewhere so we can talk?"

"I am not going anywhere with you. And you need to explain yourself." Amy started backing away from him again.

"Please don't go. Look, I know this is going to sound crazy, but I had a dream about your son, and he asked me to come and talk to you." As the words shot from his mouth, he knew this was never going to work. Why had he ever thought that this would be a good idea? This poor woman was looking at him like he might hurt her. The terror in her eyes made him question what had happened to him. Maybe the stress from dying had really caused him to lose his mind.

Amy started to run. "Help me; get this man away from me!" She screamed out to anyone who would listen.

Jack didn't bother to pursue her. Defeated, he knew she was right. He was crazy. If he ever thought for a minute that he would have a chance to convince her of this, he knew he'd blown it. It was over. It had been a mistake to try.

"Jack?"

He spun around as he heard his name and found himself face to face with Amanda. Jack caught his breath and glanced back over his shoulder toward the direction that Amy had gone.

He looked back at Amanda.

"What was that all about?"

Jack didn't know what to say. Amanda rolled her eyes when he remained silent.

"I almost didn't recognize you. What happened to your hair? You look really different, like you lost some weight." Amanda's concerned gaze flicked over him.

"Yeah, I've lost a little. It's no big deal." Flustered, Jack fiddled with the placket of his coat. *What was she doing here? How can I explain this?* Jack knew Amanda was far from stupid, and he was painfully aware of how obvious it probably was to her.

Amanda stared at him a little longer. "Are you sure? Jack, are you okay? You're not sick or anything, are you?"

Jack laughed, but it sounded strained to his own ears. "What? No, not at all, it's just what you said. I just lost a little weight." Jack glanced over his shoulder again in the direction that Amy had gone.

"Who was that?"

He remained silent, unsure how to answer.

Amanda sighed and threw up her hands, stared critically at him for another minute, and then continued down the street without another word.

What a total failure this day had become. He needed to get back to bed; the nightmares were far better than this.

Chapter 8

Amy sprinted back home, forgetting about the food she abandoned on the sidewalk. She needed to get back into her house where the world would stop destroying her. She slammed her way through the front door and deadbolted it behind her. She didn't even bother to remove her boots or her coat before heading straight for the living room and for the vodka.

How could someone be so cruel? What was wrong with that man? Who was he? How had he known about Jonathan? She wished she could take back the whole night. *Why did I think going out by myself would be a good idea?*

She put the bottle to her lips and gave the vodka a long swallow. *What does he want from me?* She took yet another long swig from the bottle and peeked through her curtains out to the street. *What if he followed me? What kind of psychopath would do that?* She checked the deadbolt again and took the bottle of vodka into the kitchen with her.

***

Brianna waited until her dad arrived home. It was close to midnight and she was tired, but she was still flying high from what Mark had said. She hoped her dad would be home soon. She needed to ask him something, but she was never sure when she would see him next. When she heard the key in the door, she jumped to open it.

"Whoa," he laughed as he stepped inside. "Is everything okay? Are you feeling alright?"

She gave him a big hug. "Yes, everything is fine. Mark asked me if I wanted to go to the movies with him."

Lawrence looked a little skeptical. "Mark, huh? You've mentioned him before. Who is this kid? Is he your boyfriend or something?"

"Da-aad," Brianna was annoyed but knew he was probably right. She had been talking about him a lot lately, but she definitely didn't want to get into *that* with her dad.

"When do I get to meet this boy?"

"You're not going to embarrass me are you, Dad?" Brianna bit her lip.

"Of course not, why would I do that? I just want to know who this kid is that's taking my pride and joy to the movies."

Brianna jumped up and down. "Does that mean I can go?"

"I want to meet him first, and he's planning on paying, right?"

Brianna was crushed. *Here we go again.* Everything boiled down to money. "I don't know, Dad. He didn't say that he was."

"What kind of gentleman is he if he's not going to pay?"

"I said I don't know if he is or isn't." Brianna pouted.

"Well, if he isn't, then you can't go. You know that, Brianna." Impatience filled her dad's voice. "I'm trying like crazy to save up some money. I still need to get you to a doctor. I'm sure as hell not spending that money on a movie with a boy."

Tears burned the backs of her eyes, and she ran to her bedroom. She slammed the door as hard as she could before locking it. *This is so unbelievably unfair. What have I ever done to deserve this? Would Mom understand if she were here?* She was willing to bet that her mom would've let her go. Mom would probably have even sneaked her a few dollars in order to go out with Mark.

She wondered if her dad would ever catch up on their bills. *Why do I have to be so different from the other kids at school and such a loser? Why am I not like them? I don't feel like them; I don't fit in with them. I'm such a stranger in my own life.* Surely *something* had to be wrong with her. She could never quite put her finger on what that was, but she knew she was different, and she hated herself for that.

She used to think she could confide in her dad about these things. Now she wondered if they would ever be close again. She missed talking to him. Would he be more sympathetic to her situation if he knew more about her and her life these days? But then again, how was she supposed to talk to him when he was always gone?

She tried to take a deep breath, but the pressure cooker of emotions was heating up now. She couldn't breathe and had to find a way out of here. She ran to her window and threw it open. The greeting of cold air opened her lungs. She pulled a razor from under her mattress and headed out on the fire escape with it in hand. Self-hatred and confusion rivaled for the forefront of her mind.

She pushed her nightgown up and pressed the razor into the top of her thigh. She winced at the initial physical pain it caused, but soon she was breathing easier as she watched the blood rush from her vein. The tension leaked out with the blood, and she lay back on the fire escape. As she felt the warm trickle down her leg, she gazed up at the stars and felt better than she had all day. For the first time in a year, she didn't cry herself to sleep.

***

Nancy was irate. Her sister had made so much progress in the last couple of weeks, and now it seemed she was back to square one. Today had been an exhausting twelve-hour workday, and she thought she would just pay her sister a quick visit before going home to crash into bed. Instead, she found Amy drunk to the point she could barely talk.

"What happened? I thought things were better."

"I tried to go out. Wanted Chineeshe. Schcarry ol' guy chayshed ne. Me. Mmmme." Amy tried to correct her pronunciation.

"What guy?"

"Dunno." Amy tried to wave her hand through the air in a show of indifference, but instead it flapped around uncontrollably. "Shaid he hadda dream. 'Bout Jonaffan."

"Jonathan?" Nancy gasped.

"Yesh. Shaid Jonaffan hadda messhage. Creepy. Chasched me. I ran." Amy tilted the bottle of vodka to her lips and drank. "Couldn't have messhage, tho. No more Jonaffan. Efvil ol' coot."

"Uh-huh," Nancy muttered, incredulous. A plethora of questions raced through her head. *Who was this guy? What in the world did he want? How in the world had he known about Jonathan? Was he even real?* She knew it would be some time before she had adequate answers to these questions. She couldn't exactly rely on Amy and her factual knowledge; she could barely string the sentences together.

She helped Amy change out of her vomit-stained clothes and into her pajamas. She tucked her into bed, unnecessarily; Amy was already passed out. Nancy went into the kitchen, filled a glass with water, and shook two aspirin from a bottle into her hand. She placed the glass and the pills on the bedside table next to Amy. Wandering around the house, she emptied every liquor bottle she could find and placed them in the recycling bin in the kitchen. When she was finished, she grabbed a pillow and blanket from the linen closet and made herself a bed on Amy's couch. Thoroughly exhausted from her day, within minutes she was asleep.

As the rising sun's rays came through the open curtains of the living room and settled themselves across her face, Nancy jolted awake, filled with dread from the night before. She jumped up to check on Amy. Still asleep. *Probably better to let her have a little more peace.* Nancy pulled the blankets higher up around Amy and tucked her in a little more before leaving her alone and closing the bedroom door behind her.

As she walked back toward her bed on the couch, Nancy glanced out the front window.

There, in front of the brownstone, was a man with his hand in Amy's mailbox. She flung the door open. "What are you doing?!"

The man visibly jumped, his limp hair plastered against his head. He held up his hands in a placating manner. "Look, I just want to leave a note for her. I'll never come back again."

As realization dawned on her, Nancy ran out the door in her bare feet. "You! I saw you the other day, parked right over there. What are you doing here? You're the guy from yesterday, aren't you? The one who chased her? Do you have any idea what you've done to my sister? You've set her back weeks in her recovery."

"Look, I don't want to cause any trouble. I just thought I was helping, but I know now that this was a mistake." He turned to leave.

"She doesn't have any money."

Jack turned around sharply. "What?"

"If that's what you're after. She's not rich or anything. And she's also married. So, whatever it is you think you want from her, you're barking up the wrong tree, asshole. So, I'm going inside now to call the police. And believe me, if I ever see you hanging around here again, I will murder you, and then I will call the cops on you again. Got it?"

The man sighed heavily. "I told you, ma'am, I made a mistake. I'm sorry for whatever harm

I've caused her; I really am. You'll never see me again."

He got into his car and drove away. Once he disappeared around the corner, Nancy walked over to the mailbox to see what he had been up to. Inside she found a blank sealed envelope.

Nancy let herself back into the house and began to open it.

"Nancy? Is that you?"

Nancy shoved the envelope into her purse by the door. "Yeah, it's just me, Amy. Be right there."

***

Amy was still throwing up. Nancy didn't know how much Amy had to drink last night, but she vomited until almost noon. And she tried not to think of how angry her boss was going to be for not showing up to work today, not to mention how much work she would have to catch up on once did she get back. By lunch time, Amy managed to eat some crackers, and for dinner she was able to keep a bowl of cereal down right before falling asleep again. She thought Amy was probably well enough to leave alone for the night, but still Nancy left reluctantly. She didn't feel comfortable leaving Amy to her own devices; who knew what she might do? On the other hand, she seemed far too hungover to want another drink, at least for tonight. Once she knew Amy was probably in bed for the duration of the night, Nancy decided to just go home. As she got into her car, she remembered the strange man and the envelope in her purse. She ripped it open and found a letter inside.

Please, before you tear this letter up or burn it, or before you call the authorities, please just know that I'm never going to bother you again; you will never hear from me again.

I don't know how to explain what has been happening in a way that you will understand, or even believe, because I don't believe or understand it myself. I don't even know how to approach this, which is why I didn't know how to talk to you when I had the chance. I shouldn't have done that to you, and for that I'm truly very sorry.

I still don't have a plan for how to tell you about the dreams I've been having. So, I'm just going to tell you about them the best way I can and let you decide if you think they have anything to do with you.

For the past few months I've been having recurring dreams. There is always a boy named Jonathan, and he holds your scarf with the doves on it. Above all, he's pretty insistent on me telling you that you don't have to worry about him anymore. He wanted you to know that he can

*swim as much as he wants now, and that he's no longer in
any danger. He really wants you to know that he is safe
now and nothing can hurt him.*

*I find it almost impossible to believe in these kinds
of things; I am a doctor, a scientist, a practical, logical man.
So, imagine my bewilderment when I saw you wearing the
scarf at the coffee shop, and then I later realized you lost a
son named Jonathan. I could be wrong, and if I am, and
I've caused you further pain because of it, I'm very sorry for
that.*

*Please know that you will never hear from me
again. However, if for any reason you feel that you would
like to contact me, please don't hesitate to call.*

> *Sincerely,*
> *Jack Parker*
> *(220) 493-8874*

Nancy shook her head in confusion. *What
does this guy want?* Goosebumps ran up and back
down her spine. She figured she'd hold on to the
letter though, in case she would ever need to share
it with the authorities. She knew for sure who
wouldn't be seeing it, at least any time soon, and
that was Amy. She had already had enough of this
guy's shenanigans.

She drove home, annoyed. She hadn't seen
the inside of her house in 36 hours, and all she
really wanted was to take a hot shower and go to

bed. She let herself into her house and immediately went to the bathroom to turn on the steam. Forty minutes later, she climbed into bed and smiled. Her bed never felt so good. She worried about Amy and wondered what she could do to help, but there was only so much she could do for her. She couldn't force Amy back into life. She had been repeatedly learning that lesson the hard way. As she laid there in the comfort of her bed, her thoughts began to drift to Jonathan. Seemingly, out of nowhere, the song "Pennies from Heaven" popped into her head. She smiled a little, hoping that Jonathan was somewhere pleasant like heaven. Exhausted and warm from her shower and hair dryer, it didn't take Nancy long to fall asleep.

The radio alarm blared through Nancy's sound sleep. Before she could open her eyes, she heard the voice of Bing Crosby in her ear. *Odd…this station shouldn't be playing Bing Crosby.* It wasn't the type of song they would typically play. It only took her a moment to realize that the song she was hearing was "Pennies from Heaven." She opened her eyes a bit and laughed at the coincidence. She shook her head. She needed to get her mind back on work. Today was going to be a busy day, especially because she had a lot to make up for yesterday.

As she got into the shower, she was still thinking about the odd coincidence, but as she shampooed her hair, her thoughts were quickly consumed by everything that was waiting for her on her desk at work. The memory of the Bing Crosby song went down the drain along with the soap that she rinsed off of her body. By the time she put the coffee on, the song had vanished completely from her mind. Work had always been her number one priority, and today was not going to be any different. For years, Nancy had thrown herself into her career as an advertising executive. That was the primary reason that she didn't have a relationship with her sister or her nephew, or with anyone for that matter; she had always been so busy with work. If she was being really honest with herself though, she knew it was the other way around. She threw herself into her work in order to avoid having a close relationship.

Guilt had been hounding her lately because she hadn't realized that her sister might have needed help before Jonathan died. She might have been able to help, or at least offer some advice, when Luke and Amy had disagreed about Jonathan. Amy probably was still right. Nancy's presence in her life would have been a day late and a buck short. She had been feeling like such a lousy sister lately, and now this recent setback wasn't helping at all. The desire to make it up to her sister burned inside her, but she was at a total loss as to exactly how she should do that. She had spent her whole life keeping her sister at arm's length, so she felt more than a little awkward now when it came to trying to help her. Amy was correct in that Nancy had no right to be indignant about Amy not leaping into her arms, but she was going to try her damnedest anyway. She would recommit her life to proving to her sister that she could be there for her.

***

Nancy thought she must have hit the lucky jackpot. Work was not nearly as demanding as she thought it was going to be, and since tomorrow was Saturday, she might actually get to stay home in the morning. Usually she worked on the weekends, but between the already-long hours at work and the amount of time she'd been spending with Amy, she thought some extra rest might be in order. Amy seemed sane and sober tonight when she stopped by to check on her. She had eaten something and decided to go to bed early, so Nancy left her with a promise to return the next day.

She couldn't wait to get into bed and put her feet up. As she turned back the covers on her bed, she noticed a single shiny penny on her pillow. *Huh. How'd that get there?* She shook her head. It must have fallen out of a pocket or something when she had folded her laundry on her bed earlier in the week. She shrugged it off and moved the penny to the nightstand. She turned off her alarm as she slid between the sheets. Maybe tonight she'd actually get another good night's rest. She picked her laptop up from her nightstand and opened it. Opening a browser window, she started to read about a new company that she had just been assigned. Bored with the content, she began browsing the Internet. Before long, she found herself searching for information on pennies from heaven. The number of people out there who made claims of dead relatives communicating with them with pennies was staggering. Her eyelids grew heavy, and she snapped her laptop closed just before turning out the light.

She tossed and turned throughout the night. Frustrated, she looked at the clock; it read 3:33. She groaned. The last thing she wanted was to be awake at three in the morning. This was supposed to be her one night to get as much sleep as she wanted. She squeezed her eyelids shut and willed herself back to sleep. Her restless thoughts kept turning to Jonathan, and she remained wide awake. She shuddered under the covers as she remembered the note from that awful man. It was entirely his fault that she was awake. What her sister needed was to let Jonathan rest in peace so that they could all have peace of their own. Instead, this man was trying to stir everything up again. She punched her pillow in frustration and tried again to go back to sleep. *Damn him.*

By 5 o'clock, she realized she was not going back to sleep. She picked up a long-ago neglected book from her nightstand and thumbed through the pages a little. When her stomach grumbled, she wondered if anyone was serving breakfast yet. She remembered hearing about a twenty-four-hour diner that opened up near her apartment. It didn't take long to make up her mind to get dressed and be on her way.

Before long, she found herself approaching the diner's door. As she reached for the door she stopped dead in her tracks, her breath catching in her throat. There, painted on the front door, was the name *Penny's*.

She shook off the feeling that was creeping up on her. *That's impossible. It's just another coincidence.* As she opened the door to the diner, she was surprised to see that she was not the only person there at such an early hour. There was an elderly woman standing at the counter paying her check.

She slowly and deliberately counted each coin as she extracted it from her change purse. The man behind the cash registered waited patiently. With shaky hands, the old woman began to clumsily close her change purse. As Nancy watched, the purse slipped from the woman's fingers, and coins spilled everywhere.

Nancy stared down at the floor. There beneath her feet was a pool of dozens of pennies. She took a sharp breath in and bent down to help the old woman pick them up.

***

As she chewed her bacon and sipped on her third cup of gas-station quality coffee, Nancy pulled the letter from Jack out of her purse and read it for the fourth time that morning. *He couldn't be right, could he?* Nancy was skeptical and didn't really want to get involved with this man who, for all she knew, could potentially be dangerous. But he wasn't the only odd thing. *What about all the pennies? Was it some kind of sign? Was it just a strange coincidence? Could Jonathan really be trying to communicate with us? And if it was Jonathan, why in the world would he be communicating with Jack Parker? Why would he involve a total stranger?* She turned it over and over, but it didn't make sense any way she looked at it.

Still, her curiosity clamored for answers. Nancy wrestled with the idea of calling Jack. *What if it really is what Jonathan wants me to do? Is there any chance of that at all?*

Already regretting her decision, she nonetheless pulled her phone from her purse and punched in Dr. Parker's number. She only listened to it ring one time before he answered.

"Dr. Parker? My name is Nancy. I'm Amy's sister. I…uh, I read the letter for Amy. Is there any way we could talk?"

Dr. Parker agreed to meet, despite the early hour. He seemed surprised to hear from her but eager to talk. In the twenty minutes it took him to arrive, Nancy thought about bolting more than once. She forced herself to sit in the booth and wait for his arrival, knowing this was probably a very bad idea. He arrived at almost exactly the time he said he would, though, and she was still there. Now they were face to face, staring at each other. Nancy smiled hesitantly before holding out her hand. "Nancy."

"Jack Parker." He took her offered hand in a gentle squeeze before he sat down. He opened his mouth as if to speak, closed it, and then started again. "I hope your sister is okay."

Nancy blinked a few times before answering. "She'll be fine."

"Look, I really don't want to be involved in this. I didn't choose this. The whole thing just kind of happened to me, but it seemed too big to be just a coincidence."

Nancy knew what he meant, but she wasn't going to share that with him. "So, what do you think is going on exactly?"

"I don't have the slightest idea. I was never really one to believe in life after death or anything like it. As a doctor, I've seen my share of death, but I have never experienced anything that would even remotely suggest that something - *anything* - takes place after death. However, it would seem that your nephew is trying to reach out to me from somewhere." Jack winced a little, as if he might be in pain.

"You okay?" Nancy pushed the sugar toward Jack as the waitress brought him coffee. "Take this. Trust me; you're gonna need it."

"Yeah, I'm fine. I'm undergoing chemotherapy treatments, and sometimes they're harder on me than others."

Nancy inhaled a little. "You have cancer?"

Jack nodded a little. "Unfortunately for me, all those years in medical school have given me enough insight to know that I'm doomed." Jack took a sip of his coffee, wincing again, this time from the taste and took Nancy's advice about the sugar.

Nancy didn't know what to say. She awkwardly fiddled with the handle of her coffee mug.

Jack set his cup down. They looked at each other for a while, neither of them knowing what to say next.

Nancy played with the spoon in front of her. "So, you're a doctor?"

"That's what my degree says." Jack's comment was clearly meant to lighten the mood. "I work mostly with the electrical aspects of the heart."

Nancy's brows rose. *Impressive.* "That sounds cool when you put it that way."

"What about you? What do you do?"

"Advertising, and it's not at all glamorous like a doctor. It's mostly long hours and bad pay." Nancy laughed at herself a little.

Jack laughed too. "There's a lot of yuck in being a doctor, believe me, but I try not to get too graphic around food. A downfall of the profession, you're grossed out by so little." He studied her for a moment. "You know, there's another aspect of the dream that maybe you can help me with. Is there a girl in your family or someone else that you knew that you lost? In my last dream there was a young lady, maybe around Jonathan's age or so."

Nancy sipped her coffee before answering. "No one comes to mind. We didn't have any other children in the family. Jonathan was it."

Jack wrinkled his brow. "She had on a pink shirt, and it had purple butterflies on it."

Nancy looked at him skeptically. "That's a lot of detail to remember, especially for a man; no offense."

Jack chuckled. "You're probably right. But that's the thing about these dreams; they're so vivid that I can remember every last detail when I wake up. That's why, when I saw your sister's scarf, it became so important for me to find out more." He grew pensive for a moment. "So, tell me about Jonathan. What was he like? Do you have a photo of him?"

Nancy began to revise her opinion of Jack. He wasn't nearly as bad as she had originally thought. She pulled her phone out of her purse and let her eyes linger on a photo of Jonathan before passing it to Jack.

Jack paled several shades when he looked at the offered picture. Nancy could tell the photo had affected him strongly. *Is it really possible that what he said is true?*

"That's him." Jack said it so quietly, Nancy almost couldn't make out what he'd said. He cleared his throat. "Tell me about him, please." He spoke to her but he wasn't able to tear his eyes from her nephew's photo.

Nancy smiled, taking the phone back so she could look at Jonathan again. "He was a great kid. He was every parent's dream as far as his behavior, and his grades, and all that stuff. He was so sweet and compassionate, which I think can be kind of unusual for a teenage boy."

Jack smiled sadly. "Sounds like a great loss."

Nancy smiled back. "Yeah, it's such a shame that it had to happen to such a perfect kid and such a great family."

"Are you and your sister close?"

Nancy hesitated; for a moment she considered lying to him. In the end, she decided on the truth. "Not at all; our family is pretty fractured. What about you? Are you close to your family?"

"Uh, I guess I would say we used to be, but my family is all gone."

"All? I'm sorry."

"I lost my father when I was young and then my sister when I was in high school. It was just Mother and me up until a few years ago and now she's gone too."

"That's really sad to lose your sister so young. Were you and your sister very close?"

"Maybe my sister and I were once upon a time, but that was just kid stuff." Jack cleared his throat and ran his fingers through his thinning hair. "So, what happened to Jonathan?" Jack lifted his coffee cup back up to his lips.

"He had epilepsy. It scared the heck out of Amy. She was worried all the time and was so overprotective. Turns out she was right to be though, I guess."

"What do you mean?"

"He'd had a lot of seizures, so she never left him alone. I know that became a sore spot in her marriage because her husband, Luke, thought she was babying him too much."

"How often was he having seizures?"

"Oh, I don't know, sometimes a couple of times a week."

"Was he on medication?"

"Definitely. Amy wouldn't have missed a single dose."

Jack furrowed his brow and stared into his coffee.

"What?" *Is he holding something back?*

"Well, it's probably nothing, and I guess it would hardly matter at this point, but from my limited knowledge and experience with epilepsy, he wouldn't have been having that many seizures if he was on the right medication. From what I understand, the seizures can be pretty well controlled with treatment. You're telling me he had them a couple of times a week, so something just doesn't seem to add up." Jack took another sip of his coffee before adding, "No wonder his mother was worried sick. I think she should have been."

"I guess in hindsight she was right. Because of that, I don't think she'll ever forgive her husband."

"What do you mean?"

"Luke left Jonathan alone the day he died. Jonathan decided to take a swim in the neighbors' pool, even though his mother forbade him from swimming without supervision."

"So that's what they think happened? That he had a seizure when he was swimming?"

"I think that's exactly what happened." Nancy waved the waitress over for more coffee.

Jack thoughtfully rubbed his chin while they waited for their coffee.

"Something on your mind?" Nancy asked as the waitress poured their coffee.

"I was just trying to work something out in my head. Something isn't right here. All those seizures even though he was medicated. Seems like his doctor would have thought that was odd and tried to look for other causes."

"What else could cause seizures?" Nancy set her cup down, interested.

"Without having ever evaluated him, it might be impossible to know." Jack hesitated and closed his mouth, as though deciding if he should go on.

"What?" Nancy demanded.

"But sometimes recurrent seizures are caused by other things, like heart arrhythmias."

Nancy stared at him as her eyes grew bigger.

"What?" Jack asked as he set his cup down.

"Aren't you a heart electrical guy?"

"Yes."

"Maybe that's why Jonathan chose you."

Chapter 9

Nancy paced around her home, trying to decide what to do. *This whole thing is just too bizarre.* She didn't really know what to even think about it, let alone know how to react. She located a bottle of red wine in her pantry and poured herself a small glass. Her hands had been shaking since her conversation with Jack that morning, and she hadn't been able to successfully calm down.

A terrible weight pressed down on her. She and Jack were pretty sure that they'd figured something out, but what it meant in the bigger picture was still a mystery. *Is Jonathan trying to communicate something to us? Is he trying to tell us that his death wasn't exactly what it seemed?* And now she was left with the bigger problem of figuring out just who to talk to. *Should I keep this between Jack and myself for now?* She was hesitant to share any of it with Amy. She was still so fragile and didn't need any more stress added into her life, not to mention she certainly didn't have any proof of what they were claiming. Still, she felt that she was keeping something vitally important from her sister. *What do I do?*

Should I go to Luke? He would probably be interested. She felt torn because of her loyalty to her sister, who would kill her if she thought Nancy was communicating with the enemy. On the other hand, Luke was her nephew's father and it didn't seem right to keep information from him simply because Amy was mad at him. *Damn you Amy. Why can't you just talk to him?*

She took a sip of her wine. Of course, there was always the option of just letting this all blow over. That looked more and more attractive by the minute. Amy never knew that Jack left her the letter, and she certainly didn't know that Nancy had secretly met with him. From where she stood, even if Jonathan was trying to communicate with them, what good would it do now? *Even if we could prove that something else entirely was going on with Jonathan medically, what difference would it make? He would still be gone.*

That was the best answer. She would just let this go and pretend it never happened. *I'm sorry, Jonathan.* She said a quick prayer for him, took her glass of wine, and drew herself a hot bubble bath.

***

Amy was hungry again. She talked to Nancy around lunchtime, and they agreed to have dinner that evening. Nancy was due to pick her up in a few minutes, and Amy was actually looking forward to the outing. It had been a week since that lunatic bothered her at the Chinese restaurant, and she had managed to all but forget about him. Hopefully he hadn't followed her home so he wouldn't know where she lived. Maybe he was off stalking some other poor woman now.

When she heard Nancy's car pull up, she ran out the door and jumped into the car.

Nancy laughed out loud. "You're in a good mood."

"I'm just hungry." Amy smiled sheepishly at her.

"Great!" Nancy practically shouted. "Where do you want to go?"

"I thought maybe that new place over on 7th?"

"You got it." Nancy couldn't have cared any less where they went. She would've driven them to the moon if that's where Amy wanted to go.

Upon arriving at the restaurant, they were seated right away, and Amy looked around the room silently for a while. Nancy gasped as she looked across the room.

"You okay?" Amy tried to follow Nancy's gaze.

Nancy furrowed her brow a bit. "Yeah, I'm fine. I just saw something strange, that's all."

Amy looked around. "What did you see?"

Nancy laughed at herself. "It's nothing, just a dumb coincidence." She helped herself to a slice of bread from the basket in front of them.

Amy helped herself to the bread, too. When Nancy nearly dropped her knife after buttering her bread, Amy looked up at her. "Are you having a stroke or something?" Amy followed Nancy's gaze and her eyes landed on a woman wearing a butterfly shirt who was headed for the bathroom.

Nancy tried to sound nonchalant. "I'm just going to run to the bathroom. Be right back."

Nancy hurried to the bathroom and locked herself into a stall. She waited inside for a moment unsure of why she went in. This entire thing was getting crazier by the minute. *What would be the odds of this woman having anything to do with the girl who Jack saw in his dream?*

Jack was too far into her head. She had to stop thinking like this. She waited until she heard the sound of the other toilet flushing, and she flushed her own. She and the woman in the butterfly shirt emerged at the same time. Nancy knew it would be a bad idea to talk to her so she kept her eyes on her hands as she washed them. The butterfly-clad woman glanced at her in the mirror and said, "Hello."

That was all Nancy needed, and she suddenly was unable to stop herself. "I know this may sound really strange, but is there any chance you lost someone close to you recently, a little girl?"

The woman looked up from the sink and gave Nancy a puzzled look. "I'm sorry? What are you talking about?"

"Please, can you just tell me if you lost a young girl recently?" Nancy cringed at how crazy she was being, and the woman hurriedly dried her hands.

"Um, I think you may be confusing me with someone else. I haven't lost a little girl. Sorry." The woman gave her a strange look and quickly exited the restroom.

Nancy felt foolish as she had to walk by the woman's table to get to her own. She could feel eyes upon her as the woman whispered to the man sitting with her. Kicking herself for making such a stupid mistake, she should have known she was reading too much into what Jack said. She plopped down in her seat across from Amy.

"You sure you're okay? You look a little bit rattled. Are you going to tell me what's going on?"

"No, I'm fine. Really. Let's just eat." Nancy picked up her menu and hid behind it.

***

Jack stood among his colleagues eating cake with a plastic fork. When he arrived at the hospital an hour ago, he thought he was going for another round of chemotherapy, but it turned out to be a trap for a surprise retirement party. The gesture was touching; someone really put a lot of thought and effort into the party. The event was catered and even some hired entertainment made appearances. The clown that usually worked the children's wing of the hospital was there, and he apparently had brought his psychic friend with him. Everyone seemed to be having a great time despite the fact that people at the hospital had been awkward around him when they learned that he had been diagnosed with terminal cancer. And most of them still couldn't help but be shocked by his retirement announcement. Like him, everyone had just kind of assumed he would practice medicine forever.

One of the nurses whom Jack had worked with in surgery for several years came over holding a plastic cup with soda in it. "Have you talked to that psychic lady yet?"

Jack shook his head and threw his cake plate into a trash can behind him. "Nah, I don't believe in that kind of stuff." He stuffed his hands into his pockets in an effort to hide what he thought was obvious irony.

"No, really, she's good. She knew things about my husband's health, and she was spot on. It was creepy." She giggled nervously, knowing that Jack was probably judging her. "She knew that he has problems with his intestines, and she also knew about his elbow that he injured while playing tennis. Isn't that weird?"

Jack just laughed. "Come on, who hasn't had stomach and joint problems?"

Fatigue was creeping in, and Jack tried to find a tactful excuse from his own party. He had never been much of a partygoer. Small talk was not on his list of strong suits, and in truth, he was exhausted from the task. His mother had taught him long ago that conversation was an art form, a skill. He had also learned long ago that it was a skill he wasn't endowed with.

He outlasted his usual tolerance for social gatherings about thirty minutes ago, but thought it was polite to stay. After all, the party was for him. It surprised him that he was concerned for the feelings of the people who had thrown the party for him. In the past, guest of honor or not, he would have grunted a few hellos and left without saying goodbye to anyone. Tonight, he was cognizant of the effort that went into the preparations of the party. He wasn't sure how much longer he'd have to be here, but judging by the amount of cake that was still available for consumption, he figured it was not going to be anytime soon. Nonetheless, he decided he did indeed need to leave. Together, the cancer and his introverted ways were a recipe for an early exit for him.

He found his coat and was heading over to where Justin was standing with an anesthesiologist, preparing to bid them both goodnight. He found his path intercepted by the psychic medium. "You're Jack, right?"

Jack smiled politely. "That's me, the man of the hour." He chuckled a little. "But I guess you don't have to be psychic to know that." He tried to step out of her way, but she moved again to block his path.

"Are you going to have a reading tonight? I've been waiting to do your reading all night."

Jack shook his head. "I know you probably think I'm rude for not having seen you for a reading, but I really don't believe in that stuff. I'm sorry." Irritated now, he tried once again to step out of her way to say goodbye to Justin.

"No, no, I'm not worried about your reading. It's your sister, Melissa. She's been all over me all night. She really wants me to tell you that she loves getting your balloons."

***

After Nancy dropped Amy off, she couldn't help but feel a little disappointed about how everything had turned out at the restaurant. She wasn't surprised that the woman in the bathroom had no idea what she was talking about. After all, why would she? Clearly, some part of her wanted to believe that Jonathan was trying to talk to them. She probably should have known better, but she let her emotions get the better of her because she missed Jonathan so much. There had to be other ways to explain all of the things that had happened to Jack and her up to this point.

No use dwelling on any of it. It was time to put this whole ridiculous thing behind her. She was so wrapped up in regret and the idea of needing to make things up to Jonathan and to Amy that she forgot all about her common sense. It was time for her to face the fact that Jonathan was gone, and she could never go down that road again. More importantly, she still had a long road to travel with Amy before she would ever trust in her again. It was time to give up chasing this ghost and time to start healing her relationship with her sister.

***

195

Jack let himself into his home in a daze. Still reeling from what the psychic told him, he walked over to the bar and poured himself a hefty glass of scotch. Now, more than ever, he had no idea what to think. He absent-mindedly took the glass and set it on the coffee table as he settled himself into his usual spot in front of the television. He stared mindlessly at the pictures as he flipped through the channels, not really seeing any of it.

He dropped his head into his hands and began to sob. He didn't know who he could talk to about what he heard tonight. Everyone in the world would think he had lost his mind. Everyone except maybe one.

He mopped up his tears with the back of his hand and called Nancy.

Chapter 10

Lawrence had a slight spring in his step as he walked home. After switching his shift tonight with another employee at the drug store, he thought he would come home and surprise Brianna. It had been so long since they spent any real time together, and he hated the feeling that he was losing her. Once upon a time, they always had dinner together, and that's when they would catch up on each other's days. They used to talk about everything in those days. When they weren't able to do that anymore, they then always counted on that time right before bed where she would tell him all about her day and everything that was going on in her life. Since he took the job at the drug store, even those precious moments were gone. Tonight, he was going to try to make up for some of that lost time.

In the few moments they could sometimes spend together in the morning or on the weekends, it seemed that all Brianna wanted to talk about anymore was Mark. It seemed that Mark was consuming all of her time and definitely all of her thoughts. Lawrence wasn't sure what to think about it, but he knew they needed to have a serious talk. He hadn't planned to have to talk to her about this stuff so soon. He wasn't prepared for boys to come into her life at such a young age. *Isn't she too young to have a boyfriend? She's only thirteen.* After all, he and her mother had been sixteen all those years ago, and he couldn't have her end up like them.

Tonight would be different, though. Tonight, they would have dinner, and they would spend every minute together until she went off to bed. He couldn't wait to see her. He had missed her company so much, and he knew that his presence would mean everything to her.

He unlocked the door and called out, "Surprise!" As he stepped into the apartment, he was alarmed to see Brianna kissing a boy on the couch.

The two kids jumped away from each other when they realized that her father had entered the room. "What's going on?" Lawrence frowned at them.

"Nothing, Dad, we're just watching TV."

"Young lady, that is *not* what it looked like to me. And since when do you have a boy with you alone in our home?"

Brianna's cheeks burned with embarrassment. "Mark and I…"

Lawrence leveled a glare at the boy. "Son, I think it's time you go home now."

Mark jumped off the couch and headed for the door. As soon as he left, Lawrence turned to face Brianna, but she had already run into her room. Right before she slammed the door, she screamed, "I hate you."

Lawrence never heard words like that from her before and the sting left him temporarily stunned. He ran to her bedroom and pounded on the door. "You open this door right this minute!"

"No! I don't ever want to talk to you again! You are so embarrassing. We weren't even doing anything!"

Lawrence continued to bang on the door. "How long have you been bringing boys up here? Is this what you do when I'm not home? I didn't raise you to be some kind of slut." Lawrence stalked to his bedroom and slammed his own door. *What happened to his little girl? Had he already lost her?* Immediately he regretted his words and knew they were largely driven by fear.

He could still hear Brianna screaming through the wall. "I hate you. I wish I had a mom and not you! You don't know anything!"

Lawrence let the sound of his little girl's words slice through his abdomen. Never in his life had he felt so wounded and impotent. Maybe Brianna was right. Maybe he didn't know anything. He stared at the blank canvas standing erect in his room. He picked up a paintbrush, and before he really knew what he was doing, he began to paint. He stood for a very long time, pouring everything out on the canvas propped in front of him. All of his problems for the past few years drained out from the end of his paintbrush. Before long, he forgot that he was angry. Three hours later, he finished his first painting in over five years. As he stepped back to really look at what he had done, he found himself looking into the eyes of his daughter. He only saw disappointment and despair.

***

Nancy pulled her car into the hotel parking lot. She still wasn't quite sure how she'd been talked into this. With shaking hands, she grabbed her purse and headed for the front doors. Her sister would be so angry with her blatant betrayal if she knew everything that Nancy was up to. Still, some small part of her thought she was doing the right thing. Luke had been so relieved to hear from her, he jumped at the chance of seeing her. Her heart really went out to him; he had lost everything, too. Even more actually.

She pulled open the large doors that led to the lobby and found a sofa to sit on. She was ten minutes early so she wasn't expecting to see him just yet, but when the elevator chimed, Luke was rushing toward her. She stood up to greet him, and he engulfed her in a bear hug.

"I'm so happy to see you. How is Amy doing?"

Nancy hugged him back. "Better, I think. She seems to be a little stronger now. I actually convinced her to go out to eat with me the other night."

He smiled sadly. "I'm happy to hear that." His thoughts seemed turned to another place.

"She'll come around, Luke. You're her soulmate. Give her time. You'll see."

"You seem pretty confident about that." Luke plopped down on the couch dejectedly. "So, what's up? I know there must be some reason you called me. Not that you need one; you can call anytime."

"I know, but I think Amy would be irate if she knew I was talking to you. I know she's being completely irrational, but I still think it's best not to tell her. Anyway, you're right; there is another reason why I wanted to talk to you. I want you to meet someone."

Luke laughed. "Trying to set me up already? I'm still married, you know."

Nancy swatted him on the arm. "No, dummy, do you have time for lunch?"

"For you, I have all the time in the world. Let's go."

They walked in silence as he followed her lead to a restaurant just a block away from the hotel. Nancy was feeling uneasy, wondering if this was indeed the right thing to do. When Jack called her earlier in the week, he had been distraught about what the medium told him. He was more convinced than ever that people from the other side were communicating with him. Nancy was somewhat skeptical, but there was a part of her that wondered. Explaining it all to Luke over lunch was a whole different animal, and she was nervous about his reaction.

As they entered the restaurant and into the large dining room, Nancy spotted Jack by himself at a table set for three. He stared wistfully at the piano player in the corner of the room. Nancy walked to the maître d and pointed to the table. "We're meeting that man there."

Luke looked over to the table Nancy pointed to. She knew what he saw: a thin, frail, slightly older man with almost no hair. He leaned towards Nancy and whispered, "He's not really my type, Nancy."

She rolled her eyes at him; he still had his sense of humor. At least someone did. Jack stood as they approached the table. Nancy introduced the two men and they all sat down.

Over their lunch, Jack and Nancy carefully described the things that had happened, and Luke listened quietly and attentively. Jack told Luke of his dreams of Jonathan and the chance meeting at the coffee shop. He delicately described to him the encounter at the Chinese take-out restaurant. Luke occasionally glanced at Nancy to gauge her reaction. When Jack was finally through, Luke spoke for the first time.

"So, even if what the two of you are saying is true and there is a good reason that you were stalking my wife, what in the world do you want me to take away from all of this?" Luke took a sip from his martini.

Nancy quickly understood that this would be a slippery slope. It was going to take some convincing to get through to Luke. He had every right to be suspicious of Jack and even angry with him, but it was also likely that this would be his last and only chance. Nancy waited, ready to help him get back on even ground if things took a turn for the worse.

Jack took a deep breath. "I think that maybe Jonathan never had epilepsy. It's possible he had a heart condition."

Luke stared at the doctor, his face turning a slow red, obviously trying to process what Jack had just said. "How in the world did you get *that* from what you just told me?"

Nancy watched Luke's anger levels rise. Jack and Luke stared at each other; Jack afraid to move, Luke too angry to. She tried to make her next comment as gently as she could in order to break the awkward and tense silence. "Jack doesn't think that someone who was regularly taking antiseizure medication would have had as many seizures as Jonathan had."

Luke looked back and forth between the two of them. "I can't figure out which of you is crazier. This is insane. You know how crazy this sounds? Even if he did have a heart condition, so what? Do you think you're doing something important? You can't exactly treat him, doc. He's dead." He took another long sip of his martini. Diners from a table over began to look their way.

Jack was rendered silent from Luke's outburst. Nancy wasn't sure what to do. She only hoped Luke wouldn't bolt. "Luke, we don't know any more than what we're telling you, but we thought maybe it was important to tell you what was going on, just in case it means anything."

Luke nodded as he waved the waitress over to pay for his lunch. "Look, Nancy, I love that we got to have lunch together, and I appreciate you guys telling me this, but I'm not sure what to think about any of it. Right now, frankly, you both sound like you've lost your minds." He walked out without another word.

Nancy glanced at Jack, and they both watched Luke leave the restaurant. Once Luke disappeared from view, Jack stared ahead at nothing in particular, and Nancy hung her head, ashamed of the pain she further inflicted on Luke. *What a horrendous mess.*

"There's one other thing I haven't told you. I didn't tell you because it's more evidence that what we're talking about is crazy, and I'm a little embarrassed by it, truthfully." Nancy looked at Jack sheepishly.

"What is it?" Jack asked.

"I recently saw a woman with butterflies on her shirt, and I regrettably asked her if she'd lost a young girl lately, and she clearly had not."

Jack sighed wearily and pointed his empty scotch glass out to the waitress.

***

Brianna and Lawrence walked side by side. Things had been tense between the two of them, but Lawrence had promised Brianna to buy her some new clothing, and he certainly wasn't going to break his promise.

After a few more minutes of silence, he finally worked up the courage to speak. "I just want you to have a good start to life."

Brianna glanced at him out of the corner of her eye, unsure if she wanted to have this conversation.

He continued, "I don't want you to make any wrong decisions at such a young age."

Brianna listened as her father spoke, and she knew his intentions were good, but he just didn't understand. *He could never understand how much Mark really loves me. Mark would never let me get caught up in a bad situation.*

Instead, Brianna hugged her dad and told him he was right. "I won't make that mistake again, I promise."

They arrived at the secondhand store where she usually bought her new clothes. It was the only place around where she could find a couple of cute tops for just a few dollars. It was Lawrence's favorite place too.

He hung back by the door while she browsed around. She worked her way through the racks, and her eye was drawn to one shirt in particular. She pulled it from the rack to get a better look at it. She liked it right away, mostly because it was covered in butterflies.

Eventually, she chose a few more shirts, and Lawrence bought them all for her. As they walked home, Brianna remembered the groceries she bought yesterday.

"Oh, guess what? I have enough groceries to make us a spaghetti dinner tonight." Brianna beamed at her dad.

He gave Brianna a bear hug with a sad smile. "I'm sorry, baby, but I can't stay for dinner. My manager called me and asked me to pick up an extra shift tonight. I only have time to change my clothes, and I've got to go."

"Are you sure?" Brianna could hear the whine in her voice.

"I wish I could, baby. But I'm already behind on rent, and your doctor's appointment is coming up. I think by the end of this month we'll have that together even after we buy groceries."

As he let them into their apartment, Brianna knew her dad would stay if he could. He looked about as sad as she felt, and she didn't want to make him feel any worse. "Okay, Daddy, don't worry. I love you. Have a nice time at work."

"Save me some of your delicious dinner. I'll be sure to eat it when I come home tonight."

Brianna hugged him and watched him disappear into his bedroom. She didn't want to tell her dad just how disappointed she was; that would only make him feel worse. Realizing how hungry she was, she tried to focus on the delicious food that would be on the table for a change. She began to prepare the meal as her dad brushed a kiss on the top of her head before he ran out of the door.

She was just helping herself to seconds when she was interrupted by a knock at the door. Brianna jumped up to look through the peephole and was surprised to see Mark standing there. She threw the door open and smiled. "What are you doing here?" She threw her arms around him.

"I thought I would come by and try to apologize to your dad. Is he here?" Mark looked over Brianna's shoulder into the apartment.

"No, he's working at the drug store, but you can catch him there if you want." *How amazing is that? Mark wants to apologize. Dad will finally get to see what a great guy he really is.*

"Okay, maybe I'll do that. Can I come in first?"

Brianna hesitated. Her dad would be beyond angry, especially after their talk. While she had outwardly agreed with her dad that day, she also knew that he really didn't understand. On the other hand, staring at Mark in her doorway, she knew that she and her dad were back in a good place, and she didn't want to risk violating his rules or his trust.

"I don't know. My dad was pretty upset last time."

"But you said he's working, right? Come on, I'll only stay a few minutes. I just want to see how you're doing. I barely saw you at school today." Mark edged a foot inside the door.

"Oh, yeah, I didn't go to lunch today because I had a test to make up."

Mark came all the way inside and closed the door.

Brianna giggled nervously. "Fine, but you can really only stay for a few minutes."

Mark put his arms around her waist and started kissing her. She was kind of getting used to the slobbery kisses, but she wasn't sure she would ever like them. He led her across the room and towards the couch. He gently pushed her down onto it and his tongue started working even more enthusiastically.

Brianna pushed him a little. "I can't breathe." She giggled to try to get some relief.

Mark continued kissing her, maybe a little more gently now. Brianna lay with him awkwardly, wondering when he was going to stop. Pushing his hand up Brianna's shirt, he inched his fingers underneath her bra. She was caught off guard, but still didn't want to stop him. She knew how much he cared about her. *Isn't this what people who care about each other do?*

After another ten minutes of his groping, she felt him pulling at her jeans. Confused and uneasy, she was pretty sure she understood his intentions, but wasn't sure that she really wanted to. *I've never done this before.* She felt awkward and stupid that she didn't know what she was doing. She was terrified, but even more afraid that Mark would notice. *Dad would kill me. This is exactly what he didn't want me to do.*

"Mark, wait." Brianna started to pull away from Mark's anxious hands.

"What?" Mark looked down at her.

"I'm not sure I want to…" Her voice trailed off.

He pushed his hand into her underwear and she could feel a sharp pain as he put a finger inside her. "Don't want to what?"

She bravely spit it out. "I'm not ready to have sex."

Mark looked at her with sad eyes. "I thought you said you loved me."

Brianna couldn't bear the crushed look in his eyes. She squeezed her eyes shut and lay back on the couch.

When Lawrence finally arrived back home, she had been long asleep in her bed. She didn't hear him open the door to check on her, and she certainly didn't hear him choke back his tears. Brianna might have been disappointed that she couldn't have dinner with him tonight, but not nearly as disappointed as he had been. He didn't want her to know how sad he was because he didn't want her to worry. He'd hoped that he was doing the right thing. What else could he do? He figured providing a roof over her head and feeding her had to take priority over spending time together. *But why then are we always so sad? I need to find a way to get my baby girl back before I lose her for good.*

Lawrence went into the kitchen and ran some tap water into a glass. He looked in the fridge and saw the spaghetti dinner that Brianna made for them. He felt the tears spring again to his eyes. He sobbed, and in the middle of the kitchen, got down on his knees and prayed. *Please show me another way; if anyone is out there, I'm listening.*

***

Amy and Nancy were seated cross-legged on the floor as their first hatha yoga class came to an end. It wasn't exactly what either of them had expected, but Nancy was feeling slightly more relaxed. She was surprised that they actually enrolled in the class and impressed that they made it through the first one. A week earlier, Nancy had been dreading going to Amy's house because she knew she had to tell her that she saw Luke.

She let herself into her sister's house and found Amy on the couch listening to the radio.

"What are you doing?" Nancy joined her on the couch.

"Not much, just wishing my life away."

Nancy put her arm around her. "Don't say that. You still have a lot of your life left. Things won't always be this dark. You'll see; things will brighten up a bit. I'm not saying they'll ever be perfect, they'll just be better. You just have to wait."

Amy looked up at Nancy skeptically and raised her eyebrows, wondering how they could possibly be related.

"So, what's up? You said you wanted to talk to me about something." Amy smiled at her.

In that moment, Nancy decided not to tell Amy about Luke. She looked peaceful for a change. Or at least she seemed comfortable. "Um, yeah, I wanted to ask you if you wanted to join a yoga class with me. I've wanted to try it for a while now, and I thought maybe it might be good for you." Nancy knew that in a million years Amy would not agree to join her, but she couldn't think of anything else on the spot.

Amy pondered for only a moment before she agreed. "That sounds nice, actually. I've wanted to find some other ways to relax ever since you poured all my liquor down the drain." Amy smirked at Nancy.

"Really? You'll do it?" Nancy was incredulous, and threw her arms around Amy.

"Sure, why not?"

Nancy was pretty sure she shouldn't push it, but she asked anyway since Amy seemed to be in a good mood. "What about Luke? Have you made any progress with him?"

Amy gave Nancy a dirty look and turned the music louder. Nancy yanked the remote out of her hand and turned the music back down, not wanting to let her sister off the hook. "I'm serious, Amy, you eventually have to put your family and your home back together again."

Amy's eyes filled with tears. "But how? My home was Jonathan. My home was him. There is no home anymore. I buried it when I buried him."

Now, as they sat in the yoga class, Nancy looked over at her sister and thought she saw what might have passed as a smile on her face.

Their instructor was a perky blond named Patty who looked like nothing got her down. Because of that, Amy had already decided she didn't like her. Nancy, on the other hand, thought they could both do with a little more perkiness in their lives.

"For anyone who wants to stay for a five-minute meditation, please feel free," Patty announced. "If you're planning to stay, I suggest staying in your seated position until we're ready to get started."

"Let's stay," Nancy said. "What's five more minutes?"

Amy shrugged silently and stayed where she was.

"Okay, I want everyone to empty out your lungs as much as you can and take a deep breath." Patty was seated in front of them and apparently ready to start.

She continued with her instructions. "The only thing I want you to do for the next five minutes is to focus on your breath. Focus on how it feels. The air feels cool on the inhale and warm on the exhale. Just focus on that. If you find yourself thinking about what you have to do when you leave here or that your stomach is growling, just put that thought into a balloon and watch it float away. Just breathe. Inhale. Exhale."

They all went quiet for the next five minutes. Amy paid attention to how her lungs filled with air and how they emptied of air. How had she never paid attention to that before? She felt herself relax more deeply, and she could feel how her lungs breathed on their own, effortlessly. She turned inward, and for the first time in months, Amy had a brief encounter with peace.

Patty broke the silence. "Okay, so here's your homework. Every day, maybe when you wake up in the morning or right before bed, or better yet, both times, I want you to take five minutes and do what we just did. Simple, right? See you next week." Patty bounced out of the room.

That night, Amy climbed into bed and stared at the ceiling. She tried to squeeze out all of the tortured thoughts of Jonathan's suffering, but as usual he was the only thing on her mind. Desperate to find even an inkling of the merciful window of peace that she felt earlier in the yoga class today, she settled in to do the breathing exercise she learned. It wasn't as easy this time, but she thought that maybe just for a moment or two it was working. She felt a brief calm settle over her, but it wasn't long before she was thinking about Jonathan again. Maybe she'd try it again tomorrow night.

The sound of her phone ringing jarred her back into existence. She had been in a deep sleep and felt slightly confused. When she looked at the clock on her bedside table, she saw that it was almost ten o'clock in the morning. *Wow*. She hadn't slept through a whole night since Jonathan's death, much less until ten in the morning. She felt groggy yet oddly refreshed as she grabbed her phone…until she saw that it was Luke. She groaned and rolled her eyes as she let the phone go to voicemail. She rolled over to try to get back to sleep, but the thought of Luke calling upset her enough to awaken her fully. In an effort to keep her anger and irritation at bay, she thought maybe she should try that breathing exercise again.

She was able to maintain her suspension of thoughts a little bit longer this time, so she stayed with it. Eventually, when her thoughts started to return, she was surprised to find that when she focused on her breath she was able to keep the painful thoughts of Jonathan away for longer and longer periods of time. The biggest surprise of all was when her thoughts started to come back in, they weren't of Jonathan at all, they were still of Luke, but she didn't feel quite as angry.

She found herself wondering how he was doing. She pictured him in his usual golf shirt and khakis. She felt a little sorry for him and for the way she'd been treating him. She remembered longingly of a time when they were happy and so very much in love. But it didn't take long for the feelings of anger and mistrust to roust any kind of compassion or sympathy she might have been feeling for him. He didn't deserve her compassion or sympathy. In fact, he didn't even deserve a phone call back. She picked up a pillow and threw it across the room. Damn him. And to think that her sound sleep was interrupted for that.

She forced herself out of bed and felt an overwhelming urge to clean something. Her house was so neglected, she realized she could probably start anywhere. Every room was filthy and in disarray. She couldn't remember the last time she cleaned a toilet. Maybe that's where she'd start, in the bathrooms.

She spent the better part of the day scrubbing, and scouring, and disinfecting. Before long she was vacuuming, dusting, and laundering until her home sparkled. Six hours later, she collapsed into a bubble bath. Her muscles ached from all the physical activity she endured, but her mind was sharp, and she felt energized from everything she had accomplished. She felt alive for the first time since Jonathan had died.

She stayed in the tub until the water became cold. She pulled on a bathrobe and wandered into the kitchen to put on some tea. As she waited for the kettle to whistle, she thought of the untouched

stack of paperbacks her sister had left weeks ago.
She took her teacup and the book on the top of
the stack and headed to bed. She stared at the
book for a while, but she didn't find it very
interesting. Everyone in the story was just too
damn happy. She wasn't in the mood to deal with
perky Patty types. Speaking of Patty, maybe she
would try her breathing exercise before turning in
for the night.

She lay flat on the bed and started
breathing. Inhale. Exhale. Inhale. Exhale.

Chapter 11

Jack didn't get a good look at the little girl's face when he heard her scream just before her head bobbed up and down in the water. He could hear the child choking as her head emerged again. Jack yelled to the girl and dove into the water from where he had been watching on a low cliff. The tides were high, but he swam toward her as fast as he could. As Jack got closer to where he thought the girl was, he couldn't find her anywhere. Panicked, he knew she must be under the water somewhere. He was not going to let this child drown, too. He dove under the water; he swam in circles and desperately looked everywhere for the girl, but he couldn't find her. Jack stayed under the water until his lungs ached. The girl was gone. He burst through the surface, gasping for air. "No!" He screamed and punched his fists on top of the water.

Jack awoke and buried his face in his pillow. He cried for an hour before he finally fell back to sleep, exhausted.

***

Brianna set her tray on the lunch table, and Mark glanced over at it. "Gross, fish sticks. I don't know how you eat those things." He picked one up and let it fall limply from his grasp.

Brianna was starving. She'd only had peanut butter for dinner last night, and anything sounded great to her now. "Yeah, these are gross." She pushed the tray away from her and tried not to cry as the smell of the food wafted up to her nose. She salivated as she watched the other kids shovel food into their mouths.

"I know what we can do. After school, we'll go to the diner and get some food. My treat. We're both going to be starving by then." Mark kissed her on the nose.

She wasn't able to concentrate for the remainder of the day at school. Between her hunger pangs and the thought of going out with Mark, it was all she could do to even sit through her classes. The last bell took an eternity, but when it finally came, she bounded to the front steps of the school and sat down to wait for Mark. She couldn't believe her luck. Not only was she going to get to spend more time with Mark, but she also didn't have to make up some lame excuse about why she couldn't go, because Mark had offered to pay. Her heart sped up as she spotted him coming down the steps toward her.

"Ready?" He held out his hand, and she accepted it. They walked hand in hand the whole six blocks to the diner.

***

Nancy shut her computer down and threw her bag over her arm. Normally she would never have left work at 5:30. More than a few people glanced up from their desks as they saw her leave. She had made such a name for herself as being a late worker that they were more than a little confused by her new erratic schedule.

For the first time ever, Nancy could see why spending time getting to know her sister and helping in her recovery was also good for herself and was looking forward to it. Nancy promised Amy she would bring food tonight, so she pulled her car in front of the diner near the hospital. As she got out of her car, she heard a commotion coming from inside the restaurant. She stepped into the diner to see what was going on.

A young teenage boy yelled out, "Is anyone here a doctor?"

A woman stepped forward. "I'm a doctor."

"We need your help here. She fainted, and I think maybe she's having a seizure."

The doctor pushed her way through the gathering crowd and toward the seizing girl. Nancy followed her. On the floor, Nancy saw a young girl, unconscious. The doctor told the boy to call 911. She checked the girl's pulse and opened her coat. Nancy froze in place, and the blood ran from her face. There, on the unconscious girl, was a pink shirt with purple butterflies.

Brianna opened her eyes and saw a strange woman staring down at her with concern. "Oh crap, did I faint again?"

***

Once the excitement settled down, Nancy stuck around and offered Brianna her cell phone. Brianna gratefully accepted in order to call her dad. She felt terrible about all the trouble she was causing him. She hoped that he wouldn't lose his latest job, as a janitor at the elementary school, because he had to come to her rescue again. She hated that she was responsible for so many of his problems. "Daddy? I fainted again."

"Where are you, baby?"

"At the diner on 15th Street."

"I'm on my way."

Nancy glanced out of the restaurant windows, hoping Jack would be there soon. She hadn't wasted any time and called him immediately when she saw the girl. "How quickly can you be at the diner across from the hospital?"

"I'm at the hospital now."

Nancy breathed a sigh of relief as she saw Jack come through the front door. He walked over to Nancy, and she introduced him to

Brianna. "This is my doctor friend I was telling you about."

While they waited for her dad to arrive, Jack began to ask her some questions.

"Does this happen to you frequently?"

Mark chimed in first. "It happens all the time. That one time in gym class, and another time when we were playing flashlight tag. One time she even had to have stitches because she hit her head so hard."

"Does it seem like it comes on when you're doing physical activities?"

Brianna nodded. "Mostly, but sometimes if I'm just emotional or excited about something." She blushed, and stole a quick glance at Mark, but he didn't seem to notice.

By the time Brianna's dad arrived, the paramedics had already examined her. Nancy listened as they explained that she seemed stable for now, and they asked Brianna's dad if he wanted them to take her to the hospital for further evaluation.

"I can't afford anything like that. I'm taking her to see her pediatrician." Brianna's dad hung his head, clearly ashamed.

Jack listened attentively. "Listen, let me examine her for you. Since I work in the hospital, I can make sure she has all the tests she needs. I'm a heart doctor; I'd like to make sure it's not anything to do with her heart."

"I don't have the money for any fancy heart doctor, sir." Brianna's dad motioned for Brianna to come with him.

"I realize this may sound odd, but I don't want any money. I just want to help her. Look," Jack took a deep breath, knowing he didn't have anything to lose. "I'm dying of cancer; money isn't doing me any good these days. Please, allow me to just do this good deed for the two of you."

"What about the hospital? Won't they want to charge me something for using their equipment?" Lawrence was obviously skeptical.

"Why don't you just let me take care of that? I've got a lot of friends over there." Jack scribbled his cell phone number on the back of his business card and handed it over. "Call me tomorrow. We should get started soon, just to be sure."

Worried, Lawrence nodded his head and he shook Jack's hand. "You're sure I'm not going to receive any bills for this? I'm telling you, I can't afford anything."

Jack patted him on the back. "Just call me tomorrow. We'll get everything handled."

Lawrence put Jack's number safely in his pocket and kissed Brianna goodbye before heading back to the school. He turned around half a block later and watched as Brianna and Mark walked off hand in hand. Lawrence absent-mindedly played with the piece of paper in his pocket and sighed. That should be him taking her home. Lawrence pondered what the doctor had said. *Something to do with her heart?* That terrified him, and he knew he would take him up on his offer.

***

The walk to the hospital the next day was bittersweet. Brianna couldn't remember the last time she and her dad had taken a real walk together. When she was little, she and Dad used to walk to school together every morning. She loved that. He used to point to the big brownstones and promised her that someday they would live like that too. Now she stared at the familiar homes, and she realized she had long ago given up on that idea. She angrily kicked at a stone on the sidewalk.

"You nervous at all, baby?" Her dad ruffled her hair a little as they walked.

"Not really. I mean, they're not going to do much today are they?" Brianna put on a brave face and pretended that her nervousness was actually caused from having to go to the doctor.

The truth was, after Mark walked her home yesterday, she hadn't heard back from him all night or this morning, and she was nervous about that. Mark probably hated her now because she was such a freak of nature.

"I'm not sure baby. My guess is they're going to hook you up to a bunch of machines and check your heart and your brain and stuff. I don't really know, but I don't think anything will be painful."

"What do you think is wrong with me?"

"I don't know, baby, but it's nothing to worry about, okay?"

They slipped into silence once again. The hospital loomed ahead of them, where it sat only six blocks from their apartment, growing larger as they drew closer. Her dad took a deep breath and held the door for her. They remained silent as the elevator took them to the sixth floor. Dr. Parker was waiting for them inside room 607, just as he said he would be.

"You're right on time." He smiled at both of them.

Her dad reached out and shook the doctor's hand. "This is mighty kind of you, sir. I can't thank you enough for what you're doing here for my daughter and me." Brianna jumped when her father gently elbowed her.

"Um, thank you," Brianna whispered.

Dr. Parker looked directly at her. "I'm sure you're nervous, so let me give you an idea of what we're going to do today. Everything I do will involve these little electrodes," he picked one up from the various machines around the room. "They're just stuck on like stickers, and the wires snap on, so they don't hurt at all. I may want to do a stress test too, to get a better read from your heart if we think that's what we have to do. Basically," he switched his gaze to her dad, "I'm going to do an ECG to monitor the electrical impulses in her heart to see if the fainting is related to that, and I'm going to do an EEG to monitor the electrical impulses in her brain to see if maybe something neurological is causing her to faint."

Brianna nodded anxiously, watching her dad do the same. Neither one of them was really looking forward to this, but they were grateful to Dr. Parker and his willingness to do such a thorough examination.

"Let's start with a CAT scan. Follow me, Brianna."

Her dad seemed kind of lost. "Is there some place I could get a cup of coffee?"

Dr. Parker glanced his way. "Second floor, cafeteria."

As Brianna lay in the CT machine, she could hear Dr. Parker's voice. "Are you okay?"

"Yeah, I'm fine, thanks." She looked up at the ominous machine and tried to forget why she was there.

"Don't worry, this is easy. Just think of something fun to do. What's your favorite thing to do?"

"Um, I like to hang out with my friends." Brianna felt awkward talking to the doctor because she didn't know him at all.

"But there must be something you really like to do. Something that really drives you?"

Brianna thought about it for a minute and realized she had long ago forgotten what she loved to do. "I like to dance, I guess. I used to take dance lessons, but we ran out of money for that a long time ago. I used to think I would study dance in college someday and maybe even dance for a living. But now there's no chance of that ever happening. Dad says it's important not to lose sight of your dreams, but I think he's kind of a hypocrite."

"What do you mean?"

"His favorite thing in the world to do is paint pictures, but it's been forever since he even held a paintbrush, as far as I know."

"I know what you mean. I used to think of myself as an artist too, a musician actually. But, that was a very long time ago." Dr. Parker paused for a long time. "Your dad's right, by the way. You should never give up on your dreams. Make sure you follow that dancing thing, unless you decide you don't like it anymore. If it's truly your passion, you'll find a way to do it."

Dr. Parker spent the next two hours explaining all of the complicated medical equipment and what each of their functions was. He tried to help her understand what each of the machines could help him find out about her. He tried to assure her that he didn't think there was anything seriously wrong with her, but that he wanted to put her through as many tests as he could to ensure that he could treat her condition, whatever it turned out to be, properly.

"How did you decide to become a doctor?" Brianna was impressed by all of the technology involved in medicine. She hadn't seen too many doctors in her life. She only saw them when she was really sick, if even then.

"I don't know, really. I guess I was always drawn to it."

"You mean when you weren't being a musician?" Brianna smiled at him.

He winked at her. "Yeah, something like that."

She started to think that maybe she'd like to be a doctor someday. Talking with Dr. Parker got her thinking about it when he told her to make sure she followed her dreams. She never thought a girl like her could ever be a doctor, but why not? For the first time ever, she started to think she could be anything she wanted if she put her mind to it and focused on it.

"This is a portable ECG." Dr. Parker attached the device to Brianna. "Leave it in place for the next 24 hours and we'll see you tomorrow."

Her dad had returned now, and was hesitant to leave. "Any idea yet what her condition might be, Doctor?"

"All I know so far is she has irregularities in her heart rhythm, but at this point it's nothing that I'm worried about. I'll know more tomorrow. Go get some sleep tonight and definitely don't worry. It's going to all be fine. You'll see."

Lawrence and Brianna walked home from the hospital arm in arm. "What do you want to do?" Lawrence threw his arm around his little girl.

"Let's go home and paint."

Lawrence looked surprised, and hugged her close. "I can't think of a better way to spend time together. Besides, I've got something to show you."

***

Nancy stood in front of Amy's front door and took a deep breath. She knew she would need herculean strength to get her through this conversation. She had second-guessed herself all morning wondering if the right thing was telling her sister about what had been happening. She still wasn't feeling very confident as she rang the bell. Not only was she going to have to tell her sister things that might upset her, but she would also have to admit to lying to her about the letter from Jack and the lunch meeting with Luke. Her sister had a lot of reasons to be furious with her. She braced herself as Amy greeted her at the door.

"Well, this is a surprise. Why aren't you at work?"

Nancy stepped into the house and gave Amy a long hug. "I have some things I need to tell you."

***

"Well, I have good news and bad news, but mostly good news." Jack was quick to add that last part. They were sitting in Jack's office at the hospital.

"Give it to us straight, Doc." Lawrence had visibly paled at the doctor's words.

"I believe what Brianna has is called Long Q-T Syndrome. It's a rhythm disorder of the heart, and it's what's been causing her to faint. There is the potential that this could have been fatal for her, but we've caught it now, and there are things we can do."

Brianna and Lawrence exchanged glances as they recognized how serious her condition was. "I'm going to start you on a medication, and I don't want you participating in any sports or exercise for the time being. I just want you to take it easy and take the medication. Don't worry; I'll help you pay for it. And Lord knows, I've got enough samples around here, they'd probably last you a lifetime."

Lawrence slumped back in his chair, relief etched on his face. "Is that it?"

"For now. I want to see how she's doing after a few months of the medication. If she's still fainting, then we might want to talk about implanting a defibrillator later down the line."

"Surgery?" Lawrence looked concerned again.

"Maybe, maybe not." Jack patiently explained. "For now, let's go with this plan."

With tears in his eyes, Lawrence stood and grabbed Jack in a bear hug. "I don't know what I would have done if I'd lost my baby girl. If there's ever anything I can do for you, please let me know."

"There may be one thing." Jack looked serious.

That got Lawrence's attention. "What is it? Anything."

"Brianna told me what a great painter you are."

Lawrence slid a glance at Brianna.

"Maybe you could be so generous as to pay me with one of your masterpieces." Jack smiled at Brianna and winked. She beamed back at him.

Jack took a deep breath before continuing. "There's also another thing I wanted to tell the two of you, more of a story, actually. I don't know how relevant it is to you necessarily, but I thought you may want to know. I think it's because I'm dying, but I've been having a lot of bizarre dreams lately, and I thought maybe you two would like to hear about them."

***

Amy was reeling from what Nancy told her. "What right do you have?"

"Amy, I'm sorry. I really am just trying to help."

"You're doing it again. Trying to inject yourself into a situation that you know nothing about. You think you can just swoop in during times of tragedy and arrogantly believe that you can just fix things." Amy was getting hysterical.

"Amy, please just listen to me. Do you think that maybe there's even a small chance that what Jack is saying could be true?"

"Why can't you accept the fact that this is just a situation that you can't fix? Just leave it alone!" Amy screamed. "Stop shoving your solutions down my throat. Just back off!"

"But Jack…" Nancy tried futilely to defend herself.

"Stop talking about him. I can't believe you went behind my back and talked to that crazy man. Who knows what kind of danger you could have put yourself into! What were you thinking? You called him? What is wrong with you?" Amy thought she had managed to get rid of that man for good, but all along he had been secretly rendezvousing with her sister. She felt even more violated by him than before.

The worst betrayal of all was when Nancy told her that she had also seen Luke. Amy didn't think that Nancy really understood how far she crossed the line with that decision. "Whose side are you on anyway? You are my sister. You should automatically be on my side. You can't afford to be Switzerland on this one. You need to decide. Now, get out of my house!"

Amy had never been so angry with her sister, but at the same time, she couldn't help but understand why her sister did what she had.

***

When Brianna returned home after their trip to the hospital, she was feeling more than a little rattled about the fact that there was something wrong with her heart. Even more terrifying was the idea that she could have died because of it. She never really gave too much thought to her heart; it was something that she supposed she just took for granted. It was scary to think that it could just give out on her at some point, and there would be little she could do about it. The thought made her shiver.

She wanted to talk to Mark; this was something he would want to know. She picked up her phone and called him for the fifth time in two days. When he didn't answer, she knew why.

Everything she had suspected all along came true in that moment. Obviously, Mark didn't want to be with her anymore because she fainted in the restaurant. He was right to not want to be with her. She was damaged, and she couldn't blame him for not wanting to take on that responsibility.

She threw herself onto her bed and sobbed. She missed him so much and just wanted to talk to him, but she couldn't make him like her again. She couldn't change who she was. She would never be like the other girls, the normal girls, the girls that Mark really deserved to be with. She screamed into her pillow as her mind filled with self-hatred.

Chapter 12

Amy was still feeling more than a little conflicted as she glared at her sister across their table for six. She wasn't sure why she was even speaking to her sister, let alone how she'd been convinced to come here. Most of Amy wanted to tell this Jack guy to go to hell, and Luke didn't even deserve the breath it would take, but the broken-hearted part of Amy wanted to believe them all and the idea that maybe Jonathan lived on somewhere. She'd give anything to be able to feel him again. Still, she couldn't help but be distrustful of her sister and everyone else at the table.

Nancy had already told Amy of the dreams. She knew they had something to do with not just Jonathan, but a young girl as well. Amy suspected that the young teenage girl seated at the table had something to do with it. The man next to her must be her dad.

Jack cleared his throat and began. "I think by now everyone knows why we're here, and if not, please allow me to explain. I think by the time I'm done, you'll realize there might be a medical reason why we're all here."

Amy believed no such thing, but she kept her mouth shut and continued to glare at Nancy. She never looked Luke's way, although she could feel his unwavering gaze burning a hole through her.

"I know all of you," Jack went on. "But let me introduce you to each other." He gestured first to Amy, to her surprise. "This is Amy and her sister, Nancy. I met them first. On my other side is Luke, Amy's husband." Amy found it hard to begrudge him the small favor of making sure she didn't have to sit next to Luke, even though it meant she was sandwiched between Jack and Nancy. "And then Lawrence and his daughter, Brianna, who is one of my patients."

Well, Amy thought. *At least I have names to go with faces.*

"Everyone already knows how we got here, but we still have to figure out why we're here. Something or someone is trying to bring the six of us together. Something must explain it, right?" Jack fiddled with his fork as the waiter filled their water glasses.

Amy turned her glare from Nancy to Jack. "I think the only explanation is that you're crazy. None of this makes any sense, and if you don't get to your point, I'm leaving." She quickly turned her glare back to Nancy, wondering again how her sister had managed to rope her into this.

"Do you have a theory, Jack?"

Amy just barely kept from rolling her eyes. *Great. Nancy's trying to help him.*

"I do. I think that Jonathan brought us all together. He started this whole thing, and I think he's going to find a way to make sure we complete it, too." Jack laughed a little nervously.

Amy was seething. "Get to the point, please," she spat out through clenched teeth.

Jack glanced over at Amy nervously. "Here's what I think might be going on, from my limited perspective. I just diagnosed Brianna yesterday with Long Q-T Syndrome. There is a small part of me that suspects that Jonathan's problem wasn't neurological at all, as his doctors had originally thought. I suspect that his problem was heart related."

"We already went through this, Doctor. What good is any of this going to do us now?" Luke heaved out a sigh.

"I don't claim to have all the answers, but I think that Jonathan is possibly trying to communicate something to us, and I think we probably owe it to him to listen."

Amy glared at Jack and stood up, knocking her chair over. "This is ridiculous. You don't have any right to say what we owe my son. You don't know anything about him." Amy had just about enough of everyone else telling her what her son wanted and what was good for him. Her fists shook with barely controlled rage.

"Except that I am convinced that he is communicating with me. Do you really want me to just ignore him?" Jack asked carefully.

"Why on earth would he communicate with you and not with me?" Unconvinced, Amy remained standing.

Jack shook his head. "Maybe because I'm dying. Maybe the veil between life and death has lifted slightly for me. I don't know. I don't have the answers to that."

Nancy put her hand on Amy's arm, and Amy sat back down. "Go on," Nancy said to Jack.

Jack took a deep breath and looked at Nancy. "I'm wondering if maybe Jonathan had Long Q-T Syndrome. It would explain all of his symptoms, and it would also explain how he died." Jack's voice gentled.

"So?" Luke appeared just as infuriated as Amy felt.

"I said I don't know. But if you guys are willing, we could probably find out." Jack looked back and forth between Amy and Luke.

"How's that?" Luke's fury boiled over. "What the hell is your point? He's *dead*."

Amy sighed loudly and crossed her arms. "And whose fault is that?" she asked acidly.

Luke's eyes filled with tears. "Yeah, I get it Amy. I know you think I killed him. I know you'd rather it was me."

Amy just turned her head away.

Jack swallowed, his Adam's apple visibly working. "There is a simple genetic test we could conduct on both of you. Then we can maybe see if that was what Jonathan was trying to tell us." Jack slumped back. "I'm concerned for some of you because you may also have it."

"Genetic test?" Lawrence spoke up for the first time as he played with the napkin in his lap.

"I'd like to conduct one for you too." Jack addressed Lawrence. "Is Brianna's mother available for the test as well?"

Lawrence cleared his throat. "No, sir. Brianna's mother died years ago. We never really did know what from. We hadn't seen her since Brianna was little. I have always assumed that the drugs finally did her in." He glanced at Brianna.

For the first time, Luke sat forward and looked interested. *Huh.* Amy frowned as he spoke. "So, you think that whatever Jonathan had he may have inherited from one of us?"

"That's exactly what I'm saying." Jack's expression looked livelier than it had all night.

"But that's impossible, because neither of us has it." Luke sounded mildly impatient.

"Sometimes, it can go on silently for many years, but it doesn't make it any less dangerous. Some of you may be at risk, and I'd like to test all three of you."

Nancy finally spoke, slowly, as if she was still processing what Jack was telling them. "So, what you're saying is, likely at least one of these three has the syndrome, and that if it's not acknowledged, they could die as well?"

Jack loosened his tie a bit and cleared his throat. "It's just a theory, but there's only one way to find out."

***

"Let's just take our minds off of stuff. I'll just come to your house, and we'll watch a movie."

Amy shrugged, even though Nancy couldn't see it. She was still pretty ticked at her sister for lying to her, but she needed a distraction now. She wandered into her pantry to see if she had any popcorn. "Fine. I'll see you in a few."

A half an hour later, Nancy and Amy pretended to watch the movie, but neither one of them felt very interested. Jack promised them the test results today, and the waiting had Amy on edge all day.

Amy crunched on her popcorn and wondered if this would change anything. She didn't know what to think. The last week had been so strange; she fluctuated between thinking she was crazy and comforted that Jonathan was somewhere around them. She felt her cell phone buzz in her pocket. She jumped up and spilled her popcorn everywhere. She looked at the phone.

It was Jack.

"Hello?"

"Amy, it's Jack. I have the results."

"And?"

"Would you like to come in and talk about them? Or do you want me to come to your house?"

"Just tell me now. I'm okay, I'm with Nancy." Amy tried to sound calm.

"Okay," Jack's voice was a bit hesitant. "You don't have Long Q-T Syndrome."

"So, does that mean you were wrong about the whole theory?"

Nancy overheard her sister and raised her eyebrows.

"No, Amy. Luke has it."

"What?" Amy nearly dropped the phone.

"Listen to me, Amy. I need to tell you that he didn't take it well. He's a broken man, and this news might have just pushed him over the edge.

He's really taking it hard and blaming himself more than ever. I know your position, but you might want to think about how you want to move forward with Luke from here. He needs help; if not from you, maybe you can find someone who can." Jack paused. "Amy? For what it's worth, if you love Luke, I think you should really consider the choice you're making. Take it from me; I screwed up the best thing I ever had. When it's gone, when it's really gone, you might regret it."

Amy hung up the phone in a daze.

"What is it? So, were we wrong?" Nancy looked confused.

Amy looked at her phone again. "I've got to find Luke."

***

Amy sat across from Luke at the kitchen table they shared for years. Tears streamed down his face. The shock of knowing that he really *had* caused his son's death…it was all too much for him to bear. "You were right. This is my fault." He sobbed as the words fell from his mouth.

Amy reached out and touched one of his hands. "It isn't. You couldn't have possibly known."

Luke gaped at her, still not sure he'd heard her right. He had expected this information to just give her more ammunition for the war she was waging against him. He had waited so long for her to say those words, but now they didn't feel anything like the way he imagined they would. There was no room to feel any of the relief from her words because he was too full from the ache of the new information about his son.

"I don't know how I'm going to get through this. This just keeps getting worse and worse. First, I lost Jonathan, then I lost you, now I'm being told that my genes are what killed him. I'm not sure if I can handle it all, Amy. It's just too much.

Amy took a deep breath. "You haven't lost me."

Luke snapped his head up and looked at her. "What?"

"You haven't lost me." Amy clasped both of his hands. "And you're forgetting one really important thing. You just found out from the doctor that you have a disease that could be life-threatening. You need to go back to see Jack and find out what you can do about it. He said it's treatable, and that's what you have to focus on now."

Luke choked back another sob. "That's the worst news of all. Jonathan could still be here with us. This was a preventable thing."

Amy nodded. "Well, we can't worry about that now. You're still alive, and we have to make sure you stay that way. I can't lose you, too."

She stood up and held out her arms to him. He jumped out of his chair and fell into them. He couldn't help but think Jonathan had something to do with orchestrating this reunion, and he sent a silent thank you to his boy.

Chapter 13

Jack finished up his final work at the hospital. He had sewn up all the matters of the genetic testing. He'd let Lawrence and Brianna know that the syndrome had not come from Lawrence, so that meant either Brianna had received it from her mother or by some other means, which, he explained to them, could happen. Either way, they didn't have to worry about Lawrence and his health. He was in the clear. Now they just had to make sure that Brianna was well taken care of. Jack insisted that he would personally see to it.

Jack flicked his gaze to the rearview mirror and took a look back at the hospital as he drove away. It was still so hard for him to wrap his head around the idea that he would no longer be working there, doing surgery there. As he drove home, dizziness overcame him. The car seemed to be spinning and he was no longer able to steer. Somehow, he managed to pull over and throw up out of his car door, but the dizziness only seemed to be getting worse. He wasn't sure if he'd be able to continue to drive home, but all he wanted now was to just get there and go to bed.

When he pulled his car into the garage, he couldn't exactly remember how he made it home.

He opened the door to his house and collapsed unconscious onto the floor.

***

Luke and Amy sat holding hands in the funeral home. Luke couldn't help but remember the last time they were in a funeral home. Amy had refused to speak to him then. That had been the hardest day of his life. As if burying his son hadn't been excruciating enough, Amy had spent the whole day ignoring him. Now that he had his hand in hers again, he knew this time he would never let it go.

Nancy glanced at them and felt pleased even though today her heart was heavy. Luke and Amy were meant to be together, and they always had been. At least that was something good that came from all of this. The more time Luke and Amy spent together, the faster the two of them would be able to heal from the tragic loss of their baby. She smiled sadly at the two of them, and she saw Brianna and Lawrence walk in. The funeral home was nearly empty so it didn't take them long to spot each other. She gave them a little wave. They made their way across the small room and sat down together.

Lawrence held a special kind of sadness in his heart. "You know, that man saved my baby's life. Seems like a damn shame that he's gone." Never in his life had anyone done the things that Jack had done for him and his little girl. He didn't know what caused Jack's life to intersect with his, but he would always be grateful.

Amy nodded sadly. "He probably saved Luke's life, too."

"And you, ma'am," Lawrence gestured to Nancy. "Somehow you were the link that put all of this together. You will always be a part of my family. I don't have any money, but if there's ever any way that I might be able to repay you…" His voice trailed off.

Nancy leaned into Lawrence and gave him a hug.

As they sat amongst each other, an elderly woman approached them; she was the only other person in the room. "Hello, were you friends of Jack's?"

Nancy held her hand out. "I'm Nancy. We didn't know him well, but he sure made an impact on us." Lawrence nodded as Nancy spoke for the group.

"I knew Jack from the time he was a baby. Apparently, he had me listed as his only next of kin at the hospital. The funeral home contacted me about his arrangements. Long time since I heard from him…" She let her voice trail off and then seemed to visibly shake herself as she remembered her manners. "I'm sorry. My name's Isadora."

***

Brianna sat at Nancy's kitchen table looking at a feast. She had never seen so much food in one place, at one time. "You didn't have to make all this food. I don't think we could ever eat it all." Although, secretly, she had a feeling they could. At least speaking for her dad and herself. Even if she ate everything on the table, she was afraid that the memories of frequent hunger pangs could never completely disappear.

"Wow, Nance, I hadn't realized you were such a great cook." Luke picked up a large bowl of green beans and began piling everyone's plate high as Lawrence passed the pork chops around. Brianna decided it was just as much a feast for the nose. Everything smelled so heavenly.

"I taught myself to cook in college. It was either that or Ramen noodles every day." Nancy sat down and placed her napkin in her lap. "So, that's it then. We are all a family now, and we will have Sunday dinners here every week until the end of time. Agreed?"

She caught Lawrence's eye as he smiled across the table at her. Their eye contact lingered for a few extra seconds.

Amy took a big bite of her green beans and spoke with her mouth full. "If the food is going to be this good every week, count me in."

Nancy looked around the table and watched her four guests - her family - hungrily eat her carefully prepared food. Life was full of mysteries, some of them unsolvable. Others, like the two practical strangers and the other two virtual strangers who sat at her table, might never be fully explained, but at least she had her chance to connect with them and have the family that she was always too afraid to have. Miracles were always waiting around the corner, you just had to be looking for them. Her real family might be fractured, but now she had this one, and she had her sister finally. Her mother Claire would probably never fully grasp what she'd missed out on.

After dinner, Brianna helped Nancy clean the dishes, while Luke, Amy, and Lawrence talked in the living room over a glass of scotch in honor of Jack.

Nancy noticed that Brianna seemed preoccupied.

"Something wrong, honey?" The strong maternal pull Nancy felt toward Brianna caught her off guard.

Brianna shrugged and dried a plate.

"Well, I just want you to know that if you ever need to talk about anything, I'm here. I know you have your dad, but just in case." Nancy winked at Brianna.

Brianna exhaled sharply. "I just can't always talk to him about everything. I mean, I want to, but sometimes it would be nice to have someone else to talk to."

"Then I guess I got here just in time." Nancy took the plate from Brianna, replaced it in the cupboard and led Brianna back to the kitchen table. "What's on your mind?"

Brianna couldn't stop the tears. Nancy threw her arms around her. "Oh my goodness. What is it?"

"There's this boy." Brianna blurted it out.

"Teenage boy problems. I can probably help with this one."

"His name is Mark, and I thought he was my boyfriend, but he stopped calling me and he avoids me at school. I don't want you to get the wrong idea about him. He's a nice guy; it's not his fault that he stopped calling me. I'm such a wild card. He probably didn't want to worry about when I might pass out again." Brianna pulled her fingers through her hair.

Nancy inhaled sharply. "Oh, honey. That is not what a nice guy would do."

***

Amy became perky Patty's prized student. She had been feeling so empowered by the classes, she found herself attending them several times a week. The hole in her heart might never be filled by anything else, but having Luke back in her life helped to ease the pain. The meditations in her yoga training were also giving her the skills to find comfort within herself when the pain from the outside became unbearable.

"Exhale completely. Empty out your lungs." Patty was sitting in her usual front and center position, and Amy gazed at her. She looked so peaceful and comfortable. Amy decided that's what she wanted for herself. She just wanted peace.

When class was finished, she approached Patty. She now knew what she had to do.

***

"Why don't you have kids?" Brianna pumped her legs to make her swing go higher.

They were in the playground across the street from Brianna's apartment. Even though it was cold out, they both still liked to be outside. They found that they had that in common. In the weeks that passed, Nancy had found herself thinking more and more about Brianna and how she was doing. She found that the Sunday dinners weren't enough time to catch up with the young girl, so she had been making frequent visits to her during the days when her dad wasn't home, just to keep an extra eye on her.

The question took her by surprise, and Nancy hesitated. She wasn't really sure how to answer it, or just how much she wanted to share. She took a few breaths and answered.

"You know, that's a good question. I think it's mostly because I decided to have a career and to really throw myself into that." Nancy pulled out her stock answer. She had said it so many times, she started to believe it herself.

"It's just that I think you'd make a really great mom." Brianna smiled at Nancy as she sailed past her on the swing.

Nancy caught her breath and could feel tears in her eyes. She stopped her swing abruptly. "You know what, Brianna? I really didn't tell you the truth just now."

Brianna looked at her with curious eyes and stopped her swing, too.

"I guess the real answer is, I wasn't a particularly happy child. I didn't want to bring a child into the world and have her be as unhappy as I was. Whenever I see a child now, I just assume they are all sad. I had to learn the hard way that people can be happy for a lot of different reasons. Jonathan had many reasons to be sad, but he was on top of the world usually, instead."

Brianna kept her eyes on Nancy's face as her tears fell.

"But even more importantly, I didn't want to become the kind of mother that mine had been. The whole idea of mothering petrified me. I just didn't want to go there." She stopped awkwardly and began mopping up her tears.

Brianna stood up and put her hand on Nancy's shoulder. "I don't care what you think; I know you would make an excellent mother."

Nancy smiled at her through her tears. "I went to work every day and I had everything I always wanted, but in reality, nothing was really working. Nothing felt like it was working quite the way I'd always envisioned it."

Brianna nodded again. "I know about that. I've felt that way a lot lately. It seems like with Dad there is always some money problem that we're having. It never feels like anything in our lives is really ever going smoothly."

Nancy touched Brianna's head and smiled at her again. Brianna smiled back.

"Have you heard from Mark or talked to him at school yet?"

"No, radio silence still."

"Did you love him?"

Brianna hesitated. "No, I don't think it was love, but it meant something. It was important in a really big, overwhelming way, but I don't think it was ever love. I'm starting to think it was a bad idea to have sex with him."

Nancy jumped up from her swing and put her arms around Brianna. "Oh honey. It was definitely not a good idea to have sex with him. You are not at all ready for that kind of thing. You are too young, and you have so much ahead of you. I can't explain all of this to you in one conversation, because it's too big, but you should never ever let a boy pressure you into doing something that you don't want to. It automatically means that he's the wrong boy for you." Nancy stroked Brianna's hair again. "Oh, you poor thing. Well, don't worry. I'm not going anywhere, and I'm not going to let anything like this ever happen to you again. You'll see."

***

Amy and Luke drove down the street together, excited to be going on their very first date together since Jonathan died. It was bittersweet, but they were both feeling upbeat.

"Where do you want to go? Are you hungry? Do you want to see a movie? Go to the park?"

"Your choice." Amy started flipping through the radio channels. Luke smiled; he missed listening to the cacophony of sounds that resulted from Amy's lack of direction when listening to the radio. She finally settled on a radio station, and they rode in silence for a while.

Amy had a lump in her throat and could barely speak. She felt like she had so much to tell him, but at the same time felt like she didn't need to. She had a feeling he already knew.

They looked at each other wide-eyed when the radio started to play "Red Red Wine."

"Do you think…" Luke let his sentence trail off.

"I would believe anything these days." Amy just turned the music up louder.

***

Brianna rode up the elevator with her dad on their way home from having a burger. She was thrilled not only to have been able to eat out with her dad, but that this time she managed to eat without making any kind of a scene. As the elevator doors opened up to their floor of the apartment building, they found two men knocking on their door.

"May I help you?" Lawrence approached the men and eyed their suits.

"Hello. My name is Jeremy Mundey, and this is my colleague Herman Schuster. We are attorneys for the estate of Dr. Jack Parker."

They all exchanged handshakes.

"What's this about?" Lawrence asked as he invited them in.

"The short version is that Dr. Parker has left a considerable amount of money for you and your daughter." Mr. Mundey set his briefcase on the coffee table. "Two million dollars, to be exact."

Stunned, Brianna and her dad could only look at each other, trying to absorb what they had just heard.

Her dad recovered first. "Is this some kind of joke?"

Mr. Mundey pulled an envelope from his briefcase and handed it to Lawrence. "I can assure you, it's not a joke. We will call you to go over the particulars, and when his estate matters are finalized, we will provide you with the money then. In the meantime, Dr. Parker wanted you to have this letter."

Dazed, Brianna and her dad saw the men out. Their eyes met as her dad handed the letter over, and she tore the envelope open.

***

As Amy looked over her yoga class, she couldn't believe where she'd ended up. Patty had trained her for the last several weeks, so that she could be certified to teach her own class. She wanted to have her own special brand, specifically for grieving parents. She thought maybe she could make a little difference in their lives. Now, as she looked at the small class in front of her, it was hard to believe that this was her life. Just a matter of months ago, she was staying home, taking care of her sick teenage boy. She never dreamed in a million years she would be sitting here now, teaching a class like this. She looked into the faces of her pupils and saw a mixture of despair and hope. She knew now exactly what it felt like to be there...and how it felt to break free.

"Good morning, everyone. Thank you so much for coming. You couldn't really understand what it means to me that you're here. I'll start off by telling you briefly a little bit about myself. Like you, I lost a child. When I lost my son, I was drowning in a sea of hopelessness. The suffering I endured was agonizing. I thought that, even if I lived forever, it wouldn't be enough time to heal from the pain. That was when I was in my worst place.

"When you're so deeply governed by your emotions, you remember the things you don't want to, and you forget what you shouldn't. My son sent me signs that I could be better, but I chose to not see them. The suffering had such a strong hold on me that I couldn't see anything else. When you're drowning the way I was, it makes it almost impossible to realize that you have another choice. I had a choice all along, a choice to drown or a choice to swim. My son convinced me to swim. And once I started, I noticed the bad memories getting smaller and smaller as I swam away from the bottom. As I resurfaced, the good memories came flooding back. I've learned that when you lose something, it helps a little to find something else. Look deep into your heart. Whatever it is that you have lost, and I mean anything, you'll find it again if you look deep into your heart. It's always there. And I'm going to show you how."

***

Isadora opened the taxi door and stepped out into the brisk winter air. She looked around the cemetery briefly before stepping toward Jack's gravesite. It was a relief to know that Jack was finally resting. She knew deep down what a hard, tortured life he had lived despite appearances. She smiled sadly as she thought of what a wonderful boy he had been in spite of the fact that his mother hadn't been what he and his sister deserved. Poor Melissa never had a chance, and Jack had only started to figure things out after he got too sick to actually do anything about it. As she hunched over the grave, she reread the inscription on his tombstone, the one carved at his final request. She wondered about it and she let the words on the stone wash over her as a strong breeze blew through her.

One can acquire everything in solitude except character. – Stendhal

***

Dear Lawrence,

It would be an understatement to say that it was a pleasure meeting you and your daughter. Your lives powerfully impacted the person I became, if only for a while. I regret that we couldn't have had more time together.

I discovered profound meaning in my last few weeks of life. I never knew how miraculous and joyful the very experience of life could be until the very end. I'm grateful that I got to sample a small taste of it.

I decided to leave you a portion of my estate, and I think Luke would be happy to help you manage this money in order to make sure it can last you for your lifetime.

Some things should be made clear to you, much of which, you probably already know. I enjoyed an abundance of wealth for my entire life but can tell you that it didn't enrich my life. I always thought I advanced through the world because I made a lot of money, but the truth is I never went anywhere. I accomplished nothing and didn't even know it. I was a virtual stranger to myself walking around in my own body. The walls that I built around me were just that. I valued them for their ability to keep me safe, not realizing they were the same things that kept everything that I could have loved out. I lived most of my life in the darkness of safety. If I had only looked up, I would have noticed that the stars could light my way. I closed every window that had ever been opened to me. I loved and lost a woman because I was a coward. I never had the fortune of having a child because I didn't trust myself to. I never had *the opportunity to truly enjoy the richness of life because I was too closed off to truly hold onto a friend.*

I am forever grateful to have been granted a new life purpose if even for such a short time. I was able to re-invent myself. I could briefly see what it looks like to be a father to Brianna and a friend to you. I could even be a brother to Nancy and Amy in ways that I never had a chance with my own sister, Melissa.

I leave you the money, not because I think being wealthy will make you happy, but because I believe that a dad like you should be able to spend time with his child. That is what will truly enrich both of your lives. The money will buy you time. Every precious moment with your child that you lose, you can never get back. If at any time you lose sight of that, which I don't believe you will, just ask Amy. She'll tell you.

Believe me; I made enough mistakes in my lifetime to know what I'm talking about. I was ruled by my past, and I walked a lonely road because of it, but you don't have to. I spent most of my adult life blaming my mother for not teaching me how to be a complete, well-adjusted human being. The truth is our mothers are not always our teachers. Our teachers can come from various aspects of our lives. For instance, you taught me to grow more in the short time I've known you than I ever learned in a lifetime with my mother. You helped me to fight back. I wasted my life believing that I was the worthless human being that my mother convinced me that I was, instead of realizing that all along I could dig deep and find the truth on my own and fight back against that.

Please help Brianna to never have small ambitions; keep her aspirations high. Even if she doesn't quite reach them, she'll still have something to show for it at the end of the day. My music may have died with me, but please don't let that happen to her.

As far as Brianna's care is concerned, she will be well taken care of. I've contacted my colleague who is an excellent heart doctor. He will call you to set up an appointment.

I don't know where I'm heading now, but I do wonder if maybe I'll see Jonathan somewhere along the way. Who knows? Maybe even our paths will cross again sometime. Until then,

With warmest regards and gratitude,

Jack

P.S. You don't have to open an art gallery with some the money, but you would truly be doing me quite an honor if you did.

***

Dear Amanda,

It devastates me, in ways that I could never explain, my lack of honesty with you when I became ill. To say that I am a coward would be a colossal understatement. As much as I wanted to tell you the truth, I more desperately needed to protect you from my torment. Our relationship, as you know, has been quite complicated. At times when we were together it felt superficial but also intimate with a deep knowingness. You understood me more than anyone in my life ever has. Either that, or your threshold for putting up with me was far broader than anyone else's. As has happened to me at other times in my life, my feelings are often deeply misunderstood. I've been accused of having an "out of sight, out of mind" approach to friendships and relationships. Ironically, that isn't often the case. The deeper I feel for a person, the more difficult it is for me to express those feelings. I have found that the best resolution was to just avoid. I have lost a great deal of friends in my lifetime due to this particular affliction.

I suspect I'm not telling you anything that you don't already know. You always seem to understand, without me having to explain - another reason why I had to let you go. You deserve so much better than to have to second-guess and figure out my temporary moods. Know that you are deeply loved and, Amanda, if I were capable, it wouldn't have been anyone but you.

With undying love,
Jack

Epilogue

The young teenager rolled his eyes and slumped against the wall. His levels of exasperation had already far surpassed their norm, and he started to get the feeling that they would continue rising. He had already been at the hospital for an hour, and all he wanted to do was just get out of there and go hang out with his friends. He knew that as he sat there they would all be swimming at the community pool and had probably snuck in a flask or two of liquor. He was well aware of everything that he had already missed this summer due to the number of hours logged in with his doctor and mother doing pointless test after pointless test. He'd resigned himself to it long ago, though, and hadn't even bothered scheming up ways of sneaking out because these days his mother never let him out of her sight.

He had spent more time in the hospital in the last year of his life than he could remember ever spending anywhere else. He never really bothered to figure it out, but he estimated that he had spent more time in the hospital than he had in school. He knew for sure that he had spent more waking hours with his mother than he had with his best friends, and that just wasn't right. He watched carefully as his mother talked to the doctor, waiting for any inkling that she was done talking, and they could just get out of there. Just when he thought his mother and the doctor were wrapping up whatever they were talking about, his mother started up with a whole new line of questioning. He slid down the wall and despairingly plopped his butt to the floor. He couldn't help but notice that his doctor looked a bit exasperated with his mother as well. *Try living with her, buddy.* He shoved his ear buds in his ears and turned up the volume on his iPhone.

He was momentarily distracted by a nurse who was running towards him down the hallway. Her hair was flying in all directions as she raced in his direction. He couldn't hear what she was saying, but it was obvious from her facial expressions that she was yelling. He yanked one of his ear buds out, curious about the young nurse.

"Dr. Parker!" the nurse called out. When the boy looked in the opposite direction, he saw a doctor a small distance up the hallway stop in his tracks.

"Dr. Parker!" the nurse was still shouting, even though she was only a few yards away from the doctor now. "The patient would really like to talk to you about his procedure tomorrow. I think he's pretty nervous."

"Which patient is that?" The doctor barely looked up from the chart he was reading.

"Doctor?" The nurse was clearly confused.

"Which patient are you talking about?"

"Um, Dr. Parker, I'm talking about Mr. Lee. We just had a meeting in his room no more than 10 minutes ago. You don't remember me from the meeting?"

Amused, the boy looked at the doctor, waiting to hear the answer to the, so far, hilarious exchange. The doctor barely glanced up from his chart. The boy thought maybe he might at least be embarrassed by the conversation, or the fact that he didn't recognize the nurse from ten minutes ago, but he really only looked slightly annoyed. He glanced back at the chart and turned on his heel. He looked over his shoulder at the bewildered nurse as he nonchalantly said, "Tell him I'll talk to him tomorrow. I've got to get home to get some rest."

The nurse noticed the boy sitting on the floor, watching, and he shrugged at her bewildered expression.

"Jackass," the boy mumbled as he stuffed his ear bud back in.

"Jonathan," his mother snapped. "Watch your mouth."

Made in the USA
Columbia, SC
04 June 2021